## "Come h
## murmured, taking his hand

They ducked under the branches and into the dark protection of the weeping willow. Lacy moonbeams filtered through the leaves. Jessica touched Wiley's cheek. He moved his head to kiss her palm.

The caress was so sweet, she was filled with longing. Jessica closed her eyes. The moment was lushly romantic. Not because of the setting. Or her mood. She felt this way because Wiley was a kindred spirit. He understood her suffering and her loneliness because he'd suffered and been lonely, too.

"I'd like to be privy to your thoughts." He nuzzled her behind the ear. Jessica shivered with desire, wanting more yet afraid.

She turned in his embrace and his mouth covered hers with a groan. Jessica felt her desire break free. Months of repression and emotional isolation spilled out of her.

Wiley crushed her close, his hands roaming over her body. "I don't want you to leave town."

Jessica froze, then gave in to the feelings suffusing her. Instantly her heat fed his and they were kissing with a fervency that left them panting. There was only need. Desire and fulfillment. Her desire and the fulfillment she found in this cowboy's arms...

And wanted to find in his bed...

Dear Reader,

Welcome to The Cowboy Club! This legendary bar/restaurant is located in colorful Red Rock, Colorado. Locals consider The Cowboy Club the heart and soul of the town. Nearly everyone has a story to tell about the place. And *everybody* has met somebody special there....

Rancher Wiley Cooper first met Dallas legal eagle Jessica Kilmer at the Club in #714 *The Bride Wore Boots* in January 1999. Of course it was love at first sight—but Wiley had to convince her to move to Red Rock. Problems arise the night Jessica returns, when a baby is left at The Cowboy Club—and Wiley must take responsibility. Will there be a happy ending for the baby, the cowboy *and* the lawyer? Find out!

I hope you have enjoyed all the books in The Cowboy Club miniseries. Come back soon for a visit!

Happy Reading,

Janice Kaiser

## THE COWBOY CLUB Miniseries

#702—LOVE YOU FOREVER
#714—THE BRIDE WORE BOOTS
#737—THE BABY AND THE COWBOY

Don't miss any of our special offers. Write to us at the following address for information on our newest releases.

Harlequin Reader Service
U.S.: 3010 Walden Ave., P.O. Box 1325, Buffalo, NY 14269
Canadian: P.O. Box 609, Fort Erie, Ont. L2A 5X3

# THE BABY AND THE COWBOY
## Janice Kaiser

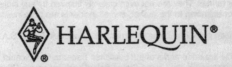

TORONTO • NEW YORK • LONDON
AMSTERDAM • PARIS • SYDNEY • HAMBURG
STOCKHOLM • ATHENS • TOKYO • MILAN • MADRID
PRAGUE • WARSAW • BUDAPEST • AUCKLAND

ISBN 0-373-25837-2

THE BABY AND THE COWBOY

... had clung to her as if she were his lifeline, as if he wanted to say "Don't you dare leave me." She'd had to pry him off to hand Nathaniel to the welfare worker. He'd had to catch hold of her arm and give it a squeeze before she'd ...

_____ **Prologue** _____

SHE CAREFULLY COUNTED the change. Four dollars and eighty-five cents—not even enough to go to the movies and she was probably the only sixteen-year-old in the world who hadn't seen Leonardo DiCaprio's latest film. Still, it was almost five bucks and that would buy milk, applesauce and carrots. Nathaniel loved applesauce. And if she was lucky, tonight, after she mopped the floors, cleaned the public rest room and restocked the shelves, Mr. Long might give her the overripe peaches she'd spotted the night before. He did that sometimes, when she worked extra hard. The week before, he'd let her have a whole sack of apples. She'd lived on them, a little milk and a loaf of stale bread for several days.

There was never enough money. It took pretty near everything she could make to pay for their room and Nathaniel's food and diapers. But even though she'd had to skip meals once in a while, the baby had never gone hungry. Not once. Her dad would've been real proud of her for managing that, she was sure.

Even so, the last month had been pure agony. She'd cried herself to sleep at night, trying to decide whether or not to give up her baby, praying she would make the right decision. When the heartache got so bad that she could no longer let the tears roll down her cheeks silently, she'd shoved her face deep into the pillow and sobbed there so that she wouldn't wake Nathaniel.

He was a good baby. Even though he was teething, he didn't cry much. And he was cute, with big blue eyes and pale blond hair—just like her dad. And Nathaniel had chubby arms that always seemed to be waving, like he wanted to say hello to the world. She was sure he'd grow up to have her father's cheerful disposition. Her dad had been like that, a good guy, always ready to lend a helping hand to a friend or neighbor. Everyone had liked him, admired him, trusted him. A lot.

She closed her eyes and sighed, shutting out the dingy little room with the faded wallpaper of yellow roses. There was only a single bed in the room, and an old oak chest with a cracked mirror over it. A pink ceramic lamp sat on a table by the bed and there was an old-fashioned ceiling light. It wasn't much, certainly not as nice as the room she'd grown up in.

Sally Anne wished she was in that room at home, almost as much as she wished that her father was here with her now. They had always been close. Her mother had died when Sally Anne was six, and it had just been the two of them until he remarried the year before he was killed.

Her stepmom, Maggie, had been okay, but it had been hard sharing her father after so many years. Her dad had been like a big rock, there for her when she needed him, always telling her to think things through before acting. "If you're going to do something, Sally Anne, do it right," he'd told her time and time again. She had tried hard to follow his advice. Only sometimes it seemed as if she either didn't know how, or didn't have good enough choices.

In fact, since the day her father died, two years ago, life had taken one bad turn after another. Lucas Springer had been the foreman at the Double C Ranch, in Red Rock, Colorado. As part of the deal, Wiley Cooper, the owner of the Double C, had let them live in a comfortable two-bedroom house that was on the property. They were a half hour outside of town, and since a lot of her friends lived on ranches, too, Sally Anne hadn't felt as if she was out of things.

But Maggie hadn't wanted to stay in Red Rock after her father died, and Sally Anne hadn't had a vote, so two months after they put her dad in the ground, they were living in Wyoming, in the Jackson Hole area. Maggie got a job at a bar and, the first week she was there, she'd met Archie. They married three months later.

Within a year, her stepmom and Archie were yelling at each other all the time, and when they weren't arguing, they were drinking. Archie lost his job and money was short. The worst was when Maggie had made her write to Mr. Cooper, asking for a loan to tide them over. Sally Anne hadn't wanted to trade on the fact that he'd been her father's dear friend, especially since Mr. Cooper had already paid for the funeral and given them money for the move.

But her stepmom knew that Mr. Cooper was a soft touch where anything to do with Lucas Springer was concerned. So Sally Anne had reluctantly written the letter, recording the words that Maggie told her to put down and leaving out that her stepmother had remarried.

Mr. Cooper had written them a nice letter and sent a couple of thousand dollars. Maggie was thrilled, but Archie kept on complaining anyway. The drinking and the loud fights got worse, and Sally Anne began thinking about running away. When she couldn't stand it any longer, she packed her little overnight case, filling it with pictures of her dad and the one she still had of her real mother, and hit the road.

She hadn't had a plan and she didn't have much money, either—just what she'd been able to save from baby-sitting. But she'd been lucky because a trucker had picked her up straight away. After that, she'd gotten a ride from Jason, another trucker who had just turned twenty and was driving for his dad's trucking company.

She'd thought Jason was cute. When they got to Boulder, he'd helped her get a job as a waitress. They'd gone to a movie a time or two, and she'd told him about her stepmom and Archie. Jason's parents were divorced, too, and that gave them something in common. He understood what it was like.

At least, that was how it had seemed at first.

Of course, she'd let him go further than she should have—a lot further than she'd ever gone before. Jason had pressured her, and she'd felt he was all she had. Besides, she wanted to feel as if she belonged to someone.

For a while, things were great. And then she'd gotten pregnant.

When she told him, Jason had given her a thousand dollars, insisting that was all he had. But he'd made it clear that she was on her own, especially since he was on the road all the time. When he told her that, she realized she'd be better off without him anyway. Even though she knew that in her heart, it still hurt. A lot. Whining about it wouldn't solve the problem, though, she told herself. She was a grown-up now, and she'd have to face this situation alone.

Her first decision was to do everything she could to make the money last. She'd kept her job right up until the time the baby came, and her plan seemed to be working. But then she'd gotten sick not long after Nathaniel was born. She wasn't able to work and she'd had to use up most of the money then. It had been all she could do to keep Nathaniel clean and fed.

Three months ago, she'd gotten the night job at the FoodMart. Mr. Long had been good to her, letting her keep Nathaniel in a basket in the back room while she worked. But there was no way she could earn enough money to keep them going long term, not when she didn't have a high school diploma.

On the day Nathaniel was born, Sally Anne had remembered her father's advice. She wanted to raise her son the right way, just as her dad had tried to raise her. And so she'd promised herself faithfully that if she couldn't make a decent home for the two of them in a year, she'd let Nathaniel go, give him up while he was still little enough to bond with other parents. He was nine months old now.

What her son needed was a place to grow up where the schools were good and the people were neighborly, the way it had been for her in Red Rock before her dad died. And then it hit her. She didn't want Nathaniel to grow up in a place *like* Red Rock; she wanted him to grow up *in* Red Rock.

It was a perfect town. Not too large and not too small. The people were friendly and always willing to lend a helping hand. Nathaniel could go to the schools she went to and attend Sunday school at the community church, as she had.

Most important of all, her dad's friend, Wiley Cooper, lived in Red Rock and he'd make sure Nathaniel was okay. That was one thing she could count on for sure. Even so, that would mean that she'd have to give up her baby forever. Just thinking about it made her feel sick and empty inside, like when Mr. Cooper had come to tell her that her dad was dead.

Sally Anne wiped a tear from the corner of her eye and took a deep breath. She'd grown up a lot in the past two years. But she didn't think she'd ever be so grown up that it wouldn't be hard to give up her baby. It would be the most difficult thing she had ever done in her life— and probably the hardest thing she ever would do. Somehow, some way, she'd find the strength to do the right thing.

That's what her father would want. And in her heart of hearts, that's what Sally Anne wanted too.

The question was, how would she go about it? How could she get Nathaniel to Red Rock? Then it occurred to her that maybe, just maybe, Jason would help her figure out a way. After all, he was the father. If he wasn't going to help support his own son, the least he could do was help her find someone who would.

# 1

WILEY COOPER TIED the reins of his horse to a tree and walked out to the edge of the bluff, where the view of the valley was best. He'd started out at first light, when the sky was barely tinged with pale gray. Now the sun was up and there was a pinkish glow on the red rocks in the distance. Most of his herd was in the deep green valley below.

He took a swig of water from his canteen. The liquid was sweet and cool. As he wiped his mouth with the back of his hand, he looked around. As far as he could see in any direction, he was looking at his land—the Double C Ranch, named for the Cables and the Coopers, who had joined their ranches when his dad had married his mother over forty years ago. Now it all belonged to him.

Wiley had always taken comfort from this land. Colorado was beautiful and Red Rock was his home. Yet this June morning, he didn't feel the peace he usually felt when he was out on the range. And he wasn't sure why.

He had awakened an hour before dawn, troubled. When he couldn't get back to sleep, he had decided to saddle up Ranger. He'd done that a lot in the past few months. Maybe these restless feelings were a sign of getting older. After all, he was going to be forty in the fall.

The hell of it was, he didn't feel old. Just the opposite. He was in his prime. His health was excellent. The ranch was profitable and the newspaper was doing well, even winning a national award for the best weekly of its size.

Being editor and publisher of the *Recorder* was a heavy responsibility, especially considering he also had the ranch to run. But he loved his work. What he was no longer sure of was how much he loved his life. Something—he didn't know what, but something—was missing.

Recently, he'd begun wondering if that feeling might be due to the fact that he was still a bachelor. Until now, he'd always been kind of glad that he'd never remarried. The notion of having a wife had been unsettling ever since he and Joyce had split up. True, he wasn't the only guy who'd been burned. But even though their breakup had been years ago and he should've been over it by now, the experience had left a bad taste in his mouth.

Not that he didn't care for the fairer sex. Wiley could dance and party with the best of them. But his philosophy had been simple—women were for pleasure, not marriage. At least, that's what he thought until he'd recently met the niece of his good friend, and the mayor of Red Rock, Ford Lewis. Damn, if Jessica Kilmer hadn't completely turned Wiley's thinking around.

For starters, he couldn't get the young widow out of his mind. Jessica was a lawyer like her uncle, and she lived in Dallas. She'd lost her husband and daughter just over a year ago and had come to Red Rock at Ford's urging to look the town over. He'd been wanting a law partner for several years, considering he was getting on in years and the responsibility of being mayor was a heavy one. "Besides," he'd told Wiley, "the girl needs a fresh start."

And, from the minute he first met Jessica Kilmer, Wiley felt like he was ready for a fresh start too. Not that all that much had happened. It was more the way he felt than anything. The irony was, he had no idea if he'd ever so much as see the woman again. She was back in Dallas, the decision about what she intended to do still up in the air, to the best of Wiley's knowledge.

Their acquaintance had started out innocently enough. Wiley had dropped by Ford's office to return a book and there sat Jessica in a light cotton sweater the color of her startling blue eyes, her dark hair hanging to her shoulders, as pretty a woman as he'd ever seen. His mouth must have hung open, considering the way Ford had grinned. The introductions were made and Wiley started thinking about the phrase "love at first sight." Of course, he was too old, and too jaded, to believe in such a thing, but the idea had kind of stuck in his brain anyway.

The long and short of it was, he'd resolved right then and there to make the most of this new feeling. So, when he'd learned that Jessica was heading back to Dallas the next day, he'd asked her out to dinner at the Cowboy Club that evening.

Jessica had been a great date. Their chemistry was good. And, for once, he didn't worry about what to say. In fact, there was so much he wanted to talk to her about that he wasn't sure he'd have time to get everything out. Best of all, when he'd told her that, she'd admitted that she felt the same.

Still, there'd been a hint of reserve in her. He wasn't sure if it was because she was still coping with her loss, or if it was because her future was uncertain. Either way, there was something awfully appealing about that sign of vulnerability. At least, it sure appealed to him.

They'd danced to a live band at the club that night and he'd introduced her to several of his friends. But the most memorable part of the evening had come afterward, when he'd driven her back to the Red Rock Inn.

"You know," he'd told her when they'd walked out by the natural hot springs spa and pool in the moonlight, "Ford's mighty eager for you to come live in Red Rock, and I've got to tell you, I'd be awfully pleased myself if that were to happen."

She'd smiled her pretty smile, her lips so sensuous and kissable, and she'd said, "Thank you for saying that, Wiley. It makes me feel welcome."

She'd stared off across the moon-dappled countryside then, the soft June air gently lifting wisps of hair off her neck. He'd stared at her, awestruck, his heart aching as he wondered whether he should kiss her or not.

After a while, she'd turned to him and said, "I've got a lot to think about, a lot of questions to answer."

That had been the moment to take her in his arms, but he hadn't. Maybe he'd been afraid of ruining the miracle of what he'd been feeling and thinking. It hadn't been for lack of courage so much as for being stuck in a trance. Jessica had touched his arm after that and said she was tired, that she needed to get some rest. Wiley had let her go with a simple, "Good night, then," hating himself for days afterward for letting the moment pass.

For a while, he'd rationalized that fate would resolve the matter. It would either bring her back to Red Rock or leave him as he was—content in the life he'd made for himself. But as the days had turned into weeks, the word *content* was getting harder and harder to accept. Although he'd only just started to get to know her, Wiley realized he badly wanted Jessica Kilmer to move there. Worse, he began to fear that wouldn't happen. The way she'd touched his arm told him there was hope, but no certainty.

A few weeks after she returned to Dallas, Wiley had found an excuse to drop by Ford's law office and see if there was news. "Got a nice note from her, thanking me for the hospitality," Ford said, "but nothing in the way of a decision."

"Got an inkling which way it might go?"

Ford had rubbed his jaw, probably to cover a grin of

amusement, and said, no, he hadn't a clue. "No telling what it might turn on."

"Hope she thinks we were friendly enough," Wiley said.

"Reckon that's not the problem."

"Think it would help if maybe a couple of us dropped her a line, making it clear she'd be welcome here?"

"'A couple of us?'" Ford said, scratching his head. "You mean, like you?"

"For instance."

Ford couldn't help chuckling. "Can't say it won't help. But I can't say it will, either."

Wiley knew he was already in danger of looking like a lovesick fool. Even though Ford was a friend, Wiley did have his pride. So he made a point of not asking Ford about Jessica again, though the old lawyer had seen him at the Cowboy Club not long after that and had volunteered that there still hadn't been any word from his niece.

Now Wiley noticed the way the sun was rising and looked at his watch. It was after six. Juana would be in the kitchen by now, getting breakfast ready. He had a full day ahead of him and he wouldn't get anything done standing on a bluff, mooning over a woman he'd only had one date with.

Besides, Thursdays were always busy since the *Recorder* came out on Friday and there was usually plenty of last-minute work before he went to press. He'd inherited the weekly newspaper from his maternal grandfather, Cyrus Cable, a colorful old geezer who'd had a saying or a word of country advice for every occasion. Cyrus's own father had settled in Red Rock just after the Civil War, and in his later years he had started the paper. Townsfolk said that all the Cable men had ink in their veins, and Wiley was no exception. Being editor of the *Recorder* kept him in the center of everything that was happening. He liked that. Yet he'd never been tempted to give up ranching to live in town full-time. Like Clay McCormick, his lifelong friend, the land meant everything to him. He was a cowboy at heart.

Wiley screwed the lid back on his canteen, went to where he'd left Ranger, and got on his horse. In spite of his ride, and his musing about Jessica Kilmer, he still wasn't able to shake his restless mood. Why? he wondered. He was basically happy. His only serious regret in life had to do with his alienation from his daughter, another sad event that he could chalk up to his ex-wife.

He'd met Joyce in college. Her family had been relatively poor, and while Wiley was not exactly the son of a tycoon, his dad was a wealthy rancher. Joyce was ambitious, determined to live the good life. Once she realized that Wiley was an honorable man, as well as rich, she had made sure he got her pregnant by lying about being on the pill.

Of course, he'd married her. Once the ring was on her finger, Joyce had all but admitted she didn't love him and never really had. Wiley had been crushed. For the sake of their unborn child, he'd tried to make their marriage work, but Joyce didn't give a damn about ranching or the country he loved. Instead, she demanded he take her to Denver and buy her a house she'd be proud to call her own. In spite of Wiley's efforts to appease her, the marriage had failed.

In the end, his family had helped solve the problem by paying Joyce off. But his ex's cold-heartedness had not extended to their daughter, Lindsay. She loved her daughter and had no desire to share her. Their agreement provided that Wiley would waive visitation rights, pay child support and take full responsibility for Lindsay's education.

As it turned out, Joyce hadn't needed the cash settlement because a year after they called it quits, she'd married Ben Larson, a rich developer, an older man who was happy to have a ready-made family he could dote on.

Wiley was back in college, trying to finish his education, when he had his one and only encounter with Ben Larson. Shortly before graduation, the man came to him, saying he wanted to legally adopt Lindsay. "You're young," Larson said. "You have plenty of time to have another family. I'll provide for your little girl as though she were my own. I love her mother and I'll be a good father."

By then, Wiley had become aware that his dad's health was deteriorating. His parents had married late in life and were looking forward to the day when their only child would take over both the ranch and the newspaper. Wiley knew his future was in Red Rock and it had been easy to rationalize that Joyce and the baby would never be part of his life anyway. So they made their deal and Wiley returned to the life he'd wanted all along.

Every once in a while, he'd get word of his former wife and child through mutual friends. Wiley had been pleased that Joyce and Ben had made a go of their marriage. All indications were that Lindsay had a happy home.

Unfortunately, that wasn't enough for Wiley to put his daughter out of his mind. There were times when he was tempted to contact her. But he didn't. Joyce had made it clear that Lindsay would be told that Ben was her natural father. Wiley realized that he wouldn't be doing his child a favor by raising the issue, so he'd resisted the temptation and tried not to think about her.

For the most part, the strategy had worked. Wiley became an inveterate bachelor. The closest he got to having any kind of relationship with a child was with Sally Anne Springer, the daughter of his foreman, Lucas. But the tragic way Luke's life had played out convinced Wiley that children and families were emotional dynamite.

Of course, it helped that he wasn't alone in his singular existence. Half his friends were bachelors—or had been until recently. It seemed as if a plague of marriages had hit Red Rock. First, Luke had married Maggie—a questionable decision, though at the time he'd seemed happy enough. Wiley's other friends had fared better.

Clay McCormick had been the second to get married. Wiley had been surprised when Erica Ross nabbed him, because Clay had been as confirmed a bachelor as he. Clay and Erica had been together for over a year now, and Clay still grinned from ear to ear every time he mentioned his wife's name.

The latest shock had been when Dax Charboneau—his best friend and the owner of the Cowboy Club—wed New Yorker Chloe James. Dax had been a certified ladies' man. Every woman in three counties had tried to rope him and Dax had evaded all of them. Chloe had changed his tune, and in record time. Wiley was still reeling from that one. Fortunately, he wasn't the only bachelor left in town though.

Two of his other good friends, Heath Barnett and Quentin Starr, were still single. Ford was, too, but he was quite a bit older and hardly counted, though Ford would not have liked hearing that. In Wiley's Thursday-night poker group, only Dax was married.

When Wiley got back to the ranch house, Juana was at the front door, waving at him. "Señor Cooper, you had a call from Mr. Lewis. He wants you to telephone him."

Wiley checked his watch. Ford was an early riser, but this seemed early even for the old attorney. He hoped nothing was wrong. "Did he say it was an emergency?" Wiley called to the housekeeper.

"No, *señor*, he said nothing to me."

"I'll take Ranger to the barn, then call Ford when I get in."

The woman nodded, and went back inside the house.

As Wiley unsaddled his horse, he wondered what Ford could want. Did he have news about Jessica? She was certainly not the only thing they'd conceivably have to discuss, though she was the subject he most cared about.

When he'd finished in the barn, Wiley walked back to the house, feeling a curious trepidation. The chill had left the air and the morning sun's warming rays were slanting down on the house where he'd lived his entire life.

Hanging his hat and jacket on the hook behind the front door, Wiley found his anxiety intensifying. If Ford had called to tell him about Jessica, he was afraid the news was bad, which in itself was a good indication of how much he cared.

Wiley went to his study and dialed Ford Lewis's number.

After greeting him, Ford let out a weary sigh. "After me, you're probably the person in Red Rock who's most interested in whether Jessica decides to move up here or not. I thought you ought to know, Wiley, that it's not looking good."

He swallowed hard. "Why's that?"

"Well, I had a call from her late last night. We talked the better part of an hour. What it boils down to is that she liked everything she saw when she visited, but says the timing may be wrong."

"So, she's decided to stay in Texas," Wiley said glumly.

"Not decided, but strongly leaning that way. She doesn't want to hold me up in case there's somebody else I'd like to bring into the practice. I assured her there's no pressure, that she should take all the time she needs. But, I have to say, the outlook isn't too good."

Wiley was silent for a long moment. The trouble was, he hadn't kissed her when he'd had the chance. Not that he'd have blown her socks off, necessarily, but it would have sent a clear signal that he was attracted to her. If the decision to move or stay was a close call for her, the possibility of a romantic involvement might make a difference—at least it would for him, if he were in her shoes.

"I hope you're wrong, Ford," he said, "but I don't suppose there's a lot we can do about it."

"I've urged her to come just about every way I know how. At a certain point, nagging becomes counterproductive. I think we're down to letting this thing play out."

"Yeah, you're probably right."

Wiley hung up, feeling dejected. He hated caring about something, but not being able to do a damn thing about it. A dozen times a day he thought of the way Jessica Kilmer had felt in his arms when they'd danced at the Cowboy Club. If he closed his eyes, he could still smell her hair and the warm, perfumed scent of her body.

Wiley got up and went to the front room, where almost every important family conversation he could remember had taken place. That was where he and his dad had spoken the night they'd decided to pay off Joyce. It was where he'd sat brooding when Luke's daughter, Sally Anne, had written from Wyoming, asking him for money. It was where, as a boy, he'd heard his Granddad Cable dispensing homespun wisdom. "Every path has some puddles, sonny," he'd often said. "A man who expects smooth sailing through life is a fool."

Wiley Cooper was not a fool. Neither was he one to let fate slap him in the face if it could be avoided. His granddad, who hadn't been a churchgoer, never would've said it, but Wiley had heard his grandmother say it often enough. "God helps those who help themselves." Wiley decided it was about time to give fate a nudge.

## 2

JESSICA KILMER had spent the afternoon in a settlement conference. It had been rancorous, draining and she was pooped. As she drove home through the North Dallas traffic, she tried to remember what she had in the refrigerator. Not much, she was sure. Over the past several months she'd gone to the grocery store as seldom as possible. The supermarket had become the bane of her existence.

It used to be that she liked shopping for groceries, but that had all changed when she lost Geoff and Cassandra over a year ago. Trips to the market were one of the things they'd regularly done together—one of their few family rituals. Jessica had treasured those times because it had been rare for Geoff to show an interest in anything domestic. He had retained the spirit and mind-set of a bachelor, remaining unfazed by marriage or fatherhood. Geoff died as he had lived, obsessed with his toys, acting more like a single guy than a grown man with a wife and child.

Jessica had never begrudged him his racy sports car, his parasailing, his Jet Skis and his golf and ski trips. In fact, before Cassandra was born, Jessica had gone along with him on a number of his adventures. Then she'd gotten pregnant and had to slow down. One of her greatest disappointments was that Geoff hadn't.

There was no doubt in her mind that he had cared for her and the baby, but in a lot of ways, Geoff had been immature. Still, he'd had a certain boyish charm that had been hard to resist. The downside was that it had some times spilled over into irresponsible behavior. In the end it had cost him and his child their lives.

After work on the fateful day that he and Cassandra had been killed, Geoff had snatched the baby from her playpen and taken her along on an errand to the super market. The authorities had said that he'd been going nearly sixty in his new Porsche when a truck had pulled out in front of them from a cross street.

Jessica felt that old pain of emptiness and loss and knew that dwelling on the past was not a good idea. It didn't make her happier, and it didn't solve the problem of what to have for dinner, either. Considering that her best bet for a decent meal at home would be to open a can of soup—not the best choice on a hot, early-summer day—she decided to stop somewhere and grab a bite on the way home.

Food had become a big issue for her. In the past several months she hadn't been eating well, and it was beginning to show. Her doctor had told her if she continued losing weight, he'd put her on a dessert diet. So, in a fit of responsibility, she headed for Mom's Pantry, a funky family restaurant on Belt Line Road, only a few miles from her house.

Jessica parked in the lot behind the restaurant and walked through the hot, humid air to the entrance. It was toward the end of the dinner hour and the place was fairly full, but no one was waiting for a table. The hostess seated her immediately in a corner booth. Jessica picked up the menu, realizing she was hungrier than she thought. Perhaps that was a good sign.

Skimming the list of entrées, she noticed an item called "Mom's Cowboy Steak." That made her think of Red Rock and the Cowboy Club where Wiley Cooper had taken her for dinner and dancing that night.

Thinking of Wiley always made her smile. He was a

nice man, quiet and soulful, intelligent and capable, successful yet humble. He'd claimed to be a simple cowboy, but she could tell he was anything but simple. The man had real depth. And he was sexy, too.

Jessica also liked that he ran the local paper in addition to his ranch. That gave him an extra dimension she could relate to. There was something else about him that she responded to even more. She sensed that he was wounded, like her. Not that he was morose or sad, just thoughtful.

What Jessica liked best was that, in his quiet way, Wiley Cooper made her feel special. She had enjoyed the evening they'd spent together and had thought of it often since her return home. In fact, that was one of the reasons she'd hedged about whether or not to stay in Dallas. Wiley had so intrigued her that she hadn't been able to tell Ford that her decision to stay on in Texas was definite.

The truth was, she didn't want to let go of the dream.

But lovely as the dream was, Jessica was smart enough to know that one night of dinner and dancing with a sexy cowboy who had a tender heart wasn't reason enough to pull up stakes and head West. Feelings had a way of changing suddenly, especially if you woke up one morning realizing that half of what you'd seen and felt had been manufactured in your own head.

Jessica was well aware that self-delusion was possible, even probable, when a woman was as vulnerable as she was. So she firmly told herself that she'd be a fool to trust her instincts. On the other hand, she couldn't deny that, since Geoff had died, she hadn't felt so much as the slightest twinge of interest in anyone else.

In the past three months she had been on four dates—twice on blind dates at the insistence of friends who were worried about her, and twice with Tommy Jack Simons, whom she'd known in law school. Tommy Jack loved to dance and, two weeks after she'd returned from Colorado, he had called to say that she'd been in her shell long enough and he was going to take her out.

They'd gone to a country-and-western bar in Richardson, close to where she lived. It had been a nice enough evening and Tommy Jack had kissed her good-night at the front door—the first time she'd been kissed since Geoff died. Ironically, though, when she had crawled in bed that night, she hadn't thought of either Tommy Jack or Geoff. Instead, her thoughts had turned to Wiley Cooper.

In fact, he had been on her mind so much that when her Uncle Ford had called a week ago, she'd been tempted to ask him about Wiley, just to satisfy her curiosity. But after reflecting, she decided against it, convinced that any decision about whether or not to pull up stakes and leave Dallas should not be influenced by a passing flirtation.

Jessica took a sip of water and decided if she wanted to eat that night, she'd better focus on the menu and order. No sooner had she scanned the list of appetizers than she recalled the spicy armadillo eggs she and Wiley had eaten at the Cowboy Club. The "eggs"—actually roasted jalapeño peppers stuffed with melted hot-pepper cheese—were delicious, but spicy. She recalled that Wiley had had the sweetest grin on his face as he'd watched her try one.

"Hey," he'd said as tears formed in her eyes and she quickly swallowed, "not too bad for a city girl."

"I might be a city gal now, Mr. Cooper," she'd told him as soon as she could talk, "but don't forget I grew up in Colorado. You can take the girl out of the country, but you can't take the country out of the girl."

Wiley had asked her about living in Dallas, the things she liked best about it, the things about city living that bothered her. She found out he'd traveled and he'd been around, but he loved his land and his life in Red Rock.

"Sounds silly, I know, but climbing into a saddle and riding over your own land is the best therapy there is."

His comment had made her think. It had been years since she'd gone riding—horses were one thing Geoff wasn't into—but Wiley's comment had made her wonder what it would be like to go riding with him. Somehow she was sure he'd find a way to make it fun for her. He wasn't the type of guy ever to make a woman feel as if she was just being tolerated.

"You decided yet?" the waitress asked, breaking Jessica's reverie. The woman was the motherly type and had curly gray hair and a faded yellow uniform.

Jessica hadn't decided, but she wasn't going to take any more time. She'd make it easy. "I'll have the cowboy steak."

After getting the rest of Jessica's order, the woman moved to the next table, where a family of four was seated. The youngest, a little boy in a high chair, was acting cranky. He was probably teething. The more his mother tried to quiet him, the worse he got, until soon he was screaming to high heaven.

Jessica tried to tune out the sound, though she'd have given anything for it to be her own baby crying. How well she recalled her joy when she'd spotted Cassandra's first tooth. There had been time in her daughter's short life for only a few precious "firsts"—when she had smiled, laughed, rolled over by herself, seen herself in a mirror.

Of course, that was all in the past now. Jessica took a deep breath to steady herself. Then, for the millionth time, she told herself that she had to get on with her life.

After a while the waitress brought her food and, halfway through her meal, the family with the teething baby left and Jessica was able to relax. Even so, she couldn't help wondering if the day would ever come when she wouldn't spot reminders of Geoff and Cassandra everywhere she looked. If she lived in a place like Red Rock, would it be worse, or better? Was the anonymity of the city good or bad for a person in pain? Ford wanted her to believe she'd be better off in Colorado, but she just didn't know.

"Honey, if you don't want to finish your steak, can I get you a nice slice of pie?" the waitress said, interrupting her thoughts. "The peach is fresh and it's real good, though the pecan's my personal favorite. So many nuts you'll be pickin' them out of your teeth for a week."

"No thanks, Mavis," she said after glancing at the woman's name tag. "I think I'll pass this time. All I need is the bill."

"Coming right up."

As she waited for her check, Jessica noticed a new customer enter and go to the counter where he sat astride a red vinyl stool. He had on cowboy boots and a cowboy hat, which he put on the empty stool beside him. The guy was tall and lean, with crinkly blue eyes and shaggy blond hair. His well-worn jeans molded his legs and thighs and his western-cut shirt was completely authentic. He was obviously a country boy, definitely not from Dallas. And even though he was young, in his early twenties, he made her think of Wiley Cooper, just the same.

As a teenager growing up in Glenwood Springs, Jessica would have killed to be in the same room with a guy like that. In fact, she'd had so many crushes on cowpokes that her mother was sure she'd wind up with one. "A baby and a cowboy by the time you're twenty, my girl," Frances had said more than once. "That'll be your fate."

Her mother had been wrong. Though Jessica had liked cowboys, she'd also liked school. And after finishing law school and passing the bar, she'd married another attorney. Frances had been surprised by that. They'd often joked about it. Her mother was now living quietly in Florida enjoying her retirement years.

Jessica looked down at the strip of white skin on the third finger of her left hand, where her wedding ring had been. She'd taken off the wide sapphire-and-diamond band the night she'd gone out on her first date, three months ago.

One of her friends, Carolyn Estes, had asked her once why she'd left the ring on so long—after all, it wasn't as if she and Geoff had had such a perfect marriage. Quite the opposite. But in a way that she hadn't really understood until now, that ring had been a symbol of the life she'd had with Geoff and Cassandra. Once she'd been truly ready to start dating again, removing the ring had seemed natural.

And yet, as ready as she sometimes felt to get on with her life, there were times, like with the teething baby, when she was so filled with longing and grief for the child she'd lost, that she wondered if life would ever feel normal again. Time, she supposed, would tell.

The waitress came by with the check. Jessica looked it over, then put a twenty-dollar bill on the table. The tip was bigger than the tab, but that was all right. Mavis probably needed it. It might even make her day.

Jessica slid out of the booth and headed for the door. As she passed the young cowboy at the counter, he turned and gave her the once-over. Then he grinned, giving her a half nod, as if to say, "Howdy, ma'am."

Stepping out into the warm, humid evening, Jessica smiled to herself. She was reminded of a time long, long ago—the occasion of her first visit to Red Rock. She'd been only fifteen at the time, her father having died a few months earlier from complications following routine surgery. She and her mother had gone to stay with Ford for a while. The evening they arrived, her uncle had taken them to the Cowboy Club for dinner.

Jessica recalled every moment of that night. Her mouth had dropped open when she had stepped inside the authentic Wild West bar and restaurant. Queued up to the mile-long mahogany bar, shoulder to shoulder, was the longest, best-looking lineup of cowboys she'd ever seen in her life.

Frances had been so wrapped up in her loss that she was understandably oblivious to Jessica's interest in the men, but Ford must have noticed because when they were told that they'd have to wait for a table, he'd asked if she wanted to get a Coke at the bar. Boy, did she ever! Even now Jessica recalled the way she'd sashayed over to the bartender and ordered her drink, trying hard to act grown-up and hoping that at least one of the cowboys would think she was seventeen or eighteen, instead of barely having turned fifteen.

Sexy as those cowboys were, though, something else had happened to her that night—something that had changed her forever. Once they were seated at a table, Jessica'd been pretty much forced to listen to what Ford was saying. The longer he talked, the more she began to appreciate how he was helping her mother sort out the legal and financial quagmire she found herself in when her husband had died. Right then, Jessica decided that she would be a lawyer, too. She wanted to help people who had problems, to make their lives easier and better, the way her Uncle Ford was helping them.

Now Jessica got in her car and started the engine, grateful for the cool whoosh from the air conditioner. Gripping the steering wheel, she stared out the windshield at the twilight. She felt better for having eaten, but the prospect of returning to her empty house did not make for the happiest of thoughts. But that was her life now—alone, no baby, no husband.

Jessica shook her head, determined not to let herself get depressed. She was an intelligent woman, in control of her own destiny. It was up to her to make sure her thoughts were as pleasant as possible. Perhaps even about good-looking cowboys—like Wiley Cooper, for instance.

WILEY COOPER SAT in his rental car across the street from Jessica Kilmer's modern white brick rancher. Nearly two hours had passed since he'd found the house and parked his car. There was still no sign of her. Of course, he'd known he was taking a calculated risk in coming to Dallas without warning, much less an invitation. And he knew he might come across as a fool, considering how briefly they'd known each other. But he had decided to go for broke. He also figured his best chance of getting an honest response was if he caught her unprepared. That wasn't very considerate, he knew, but this was one instance when truth was the most important thing—the truth he wished to impart as well as the truth he hoped to glean from her reaction to him.

What he hadn't counted on was that she might not be coming home. For all he knew, Jessica could be away on a business trip, or worse, she might be staying with somebody else.

Like a boyfriend.

She hadn't given him even the slightest indication that she was dating anyone, but then, neither had she had any obligation to do so. Even so it seemed unlikely she would have been so engaging that night at the Cowboy Club if she'd had someone special back home. Still, she could have gotten involved with some guy since her return to Dallas. Anything was possible.

Wiley shook his head. He wasn't doing himself any good being negative. Or being foolish, for that matter.

When he came right down to it, Wiley knew he was acting like a nervous teenager.

Hell's bells. What was happening to him? For the first
time in ages he was nervous and ill-at-ease over the prospect of seeing a woman. That was stupid. Or was it? Jessica had seemed pretty special. The truth was, she'd
stirred something in him, something deep. She had made
him care again.

When was the last time he'd felt this way, really had a
crush on somebody, for heaven's sake? Not since he was
a kid, that was for sure. The big difference now was that
he was a man. That meant, in spite of the way he felt inside, he could control his actions. Make things happen
the way he wanted.

Or could he?

Well, he could at least give it his best shot. That much
he knew he could count on. Which explained why he was
here in the first place. He simply would not let this
woman slip away without a fight. And that was what
he'd come to tell her.

As he stared at the twilight through the boughs of the
large red mulberry tree in front of her house, a car came
up the street and pulled into her driveway. Wiley sat upright. When he saw her get out of the car, he opened his
door. Jessica, a bulging black leather briefcase in hand
and suit jacket over her arm, walked around the vehicle,
turning as she saw him crossing the street. The light was
still good enough for him to see the surprise on her face.

"Evening, Jessica," he said, tipping his Stetson. "Wiley
Cooper from Red Rock. Just happened to be in the neighborhood and thought I'd drop by and say hello."

The surprise on her face had changed to something
bordering on delight. He was encouraged.

"Just happened to be in the neighborhood, huh?"

"The prettier the lady, the longer the detour a fella's
willing to make."

"I guess I should feel flattered."

"I reckon so," he said, her smile encouraging him further.

"Seriously, what are you doing in Dallas?"

"If I didn't say I came to see you, I'd be lying."

She hesitated, searching his eyes. "Really?"

"Yes, ma'am. I know it's not very considerate dropping in uninvited," he added, wanting her to understand his motivation now that it looked as if he was making progress, "but I didn't want to make a big deal of it. And, to be honest, I wanted to catch you unprepared."

"You certainly succeeded in that."

"We can talk out here if you'd feel more comfortable. It's a nice evening."

Jessica glanced up at the sky, the line of her neck visible in the shadowed light. Her dark hair was twisted up, the skin under the open neck of her blouse inviting. The scent of her perfume reminded him of the evening they'd danced. His heart beat a little harder with nervous anticipation. She looked straight into his eyes.

"Give me a hint what it is you want to talk about," she said cautiously.

"To be frank, I'm a self-appointed, one-man delegation that's come to try to convince you to move to Red Rock."

"Oh?" she said, looking pleased.

"I know that's coming on pretty strong, but there are some things that just have to be said, especially when the conviction's strong."

"I'm flattered that you'd come all the way down here to say that, Wiley. But I hope you have other business in Dallas, as well."

"You're all the reason I needed, Jessica," he said, his voice low but strong. "I'm convinced it'd be a terrible shame if you didn't give Red Rock a try."

She studied him for a while, apparently thinking.

When she finally spoke, her voice was tentative. "Why is that, Wiley?"

He stared at her unflinchingly. "Honestly?"

"Yes, honestly." She set her briefcase down on the walk beside her and waited for his reply.

"First, that evening we were together at the Cowboy Club was one of the most enjoyable I've spent in years."

"I enjoyed it, too."

"Second, it ended on a disappointing note."

"Disappointing?"

"I should have kissed you and I didn't."

Jessica looked down at her shoes, seemingly embarrassed by his directness.

"I've been regretting it ever since," he added.

She was silent, still not looking at him.

"I hope I don't embarrass you by saying that."

She shook her head, biting her lip. "No, not at all."

He reached out then and touched her cheek with the tips of his fingers, causing her to lift her eyes. Then, taking off his hat, he moved forward, lowered his face and gently pressed his lips to hers. Jessica let him kiss her for a long moment before easing back. Again, she lowered her eyes, shifting uncomfortably before looking up at him.

"I don't know what to say."

"Well, I say better late than never," he replied amiably.

Jessica laughed. "I don't know when I've been more surprised." She smiled sweetly. "Well, I'm not being very hospitable, am I? Would you care to come in? I'd offer you some dessert, but I don't think I've even got ice cream. A trip to the grocery store is overdue. I think I could manage a pot of coffee, though, if that would interest you."

"Thank you kindly, but I think I've already imposed enough. I am going to be in town until day after tomorrow, though. You wouldn't be free for dinner tomorrow night by any chance, would you?"

"Yes, I am free."

"Great. What time can I pick you up?"

"Seven?"

"Suits me fine."

"Then tomorrow at seven," she said, sounding pleased. She leaned down and picked up her briefcase, draping her suit jacket over it. She extended her right hand toward him. "I'm really glad you came, Wiley."

He took her slender hand, giving it a firm squeeze. Then he leaned forward again and kissed her on the cheek. "So am I," he whispered in her ear. Putting his hat back on his head, he started across the street to his rental car. His step felt so light he was practically floating.

Jessica was at the entrance to her house as he pulled his car door open. She gave him a little wave and he waved back. Once inside the car, Wiley gave a yelp of glee and started the engine. She was already inside, but he stared at her door for a moment or two anyway. He could feel it in his bones. Coming to Dallas had been the right thing to do.

# 3

JESSICA WAS FORTUNATE to have an easy day at work. Mostly she did paperwork, drafted a few letters and managed to sneak out of the office early. She wanted to swing by the supermarket and pick up something to snack on with the cocktail she would offer before they headed out. She didn't have much in the house to drink. There might have been a can or two of imported beer, perhaps a bottle of Merlot, but that was pretty much it.

She decided to get a nice California Chardonnay and some small bottles of hard liquor. She'd never been much of a drinker, though Geoff had indulged on occasion, if he'd had a hard day at work or if he was celebrating. She had given away their stock of liquor after the accident, but she realized now that it wasn't a bad idea to have something around for guests. Of course, she couldn't imagine who she'd invite, apart from her friend, Carolyn. But then, life was full of surprises—Wiley coming to Dallas, for example.

Jessica still couldn't get over that he had come all the way to Texas simply to encourage her to move to Red Rock. It was probably the most flattering thing any man had ever done. Geoff had had his charms, but he'd never made her feel truly special, not the way Wiley's surprise visit had.

His being here would take some getting used to, but it would be a nice change to have to adjust to something pleasant. Besides, she had a feeling that Wiley would find a way to make it easy for her. There was something about him that made him comfortable to be around. She wasn't sure what it was, unless it was that he was at ease with himself.

Not that the man didn't have problems of his own— that wounded streak she'd sensed in him, for example. But Wiley Cooper was a mature man who knew who he was. He understood his role in life and his place in his community. That was rare. It was kind of alluring, too. At least, it had gotten her heart to ticking.

From their conversation that night in Red Rock, and also from the things her uncle had said, she'd learned that Wiley had been leading a life almost as lonely as hers, though, of course, he'd had a lot more years to adjust. "I didn't think any woman alive could draw Wiley out of his shell," Ford had told her. "But you sure seem to have gotten his attention."

At the time, she'd dismissed her uncle's comment as another ploy in his campaign to lure her to Red Rock. More than once in the past twenty-four hours she'd wondered if Ford hadn't put Wiley up to this trip to Dallas. In the end, she concluded that neither her uncle nor Wiley could be that manipulative.

Still, that didn't explain what Wiley expected. Or, for that matter, what her own expectations were. Both were important issues that would have to be sorted out down the road. For now, all she could say for sure was that she was very much looking forward to having dinner with him.

She checked her watch as she made her way up Highway 75, headed for Richardson. She had plenty of time, though she wanted to bathe and change before going out. About an hour before she'd left the office, Wiley had called to say that he'd made reservations at Nero's on Lower Greenville. That particular restaurant brought back memories—the kind of memories she didn't want to dwell on. But she knew that wasn't Wiley's fault. It had been awfully considerate of him to tell her where they were going so she'd know how to dress.

"It's a very fancy place," she'd said, trying to keep the emotion out of her voice. "I'd be happy with someplace a lot more modest." The truth was, Geoff had taken her to Nero's to celebrate the day that they'd found out she was pregnant with Cassandra.

"But being with you again is a special occasion," Wiley had replied. "And the concierge at my hotel recommended it highly."

She was also surprised to learn that he was staying at the Crescent Hotel, which didn't seem the sort of place for a cowboy, though, she reminded herself, Wiley was a well-to-do rancher, who also owned a newspaper. "One of the most respected men in the entire county," was the way Ford had described him. It went without saying that he was well off, too, though to Wiley's credit, he didn't flaunt it.

Jessica exited the highway and made her way on the surface streets to the market where she always shopped. Though she felt her usual twinge when she pulled into the parking spot out front, she hopped out of the car and went inside with uncommon resolve, almost indifferent to the painful associations.

She bought some cheese and crackers and a tray of crudités from the deli. Then she picked up some beer and wine, deciding to skip the hard liquor, after all. So focused was she on the evening ahead that she didn't give her usual anxious look down the aisle where the diapers and baby food were kept. Nor did she think about the ice-cream aisle, Geoff's favorite haunt.

As soon as she got home, she ran a bath, put away everything she'd bought at the store, stripped down and hopped into the tub. The bubbles felt sensuous on her skin. As she started to relax in the warm water, her mind drifted back to Wiley's kiss. The look of sweet determination in his eyes just before his lips touched hers had been in her thoughts on and off all day. For all his gentleness, Wiley was a man who knew exactly what he wanted. That, and his audaciousness, intrigued her.

Just thinking about him, Jessica began to feel aroused. She ran her hands over her breasts and stomach and up and down her thighs. It had been over a year since she'd had sex and just as long since she'd given it more than a passing thought. Yet in spite of that, she found herself feeling tingly. The anticipation of an evening with Wiley was turning her on, which said something important about her feelings for him. Either that, or it was a sign of how long she'd been without a man.

Jessica didn't have much time until he arrived, so she cut her bath short. As she dried herself off, she really looked at her body in the mirror for the first time in months and months. The doctor was right. She was a little on the thin side. But she felt vibrant, more alive than at any time she could recall, except for her evening of dinner and dancing with Wiley at the Cowboy Club, that is. If he had felt even a little of the magic she'd felt that night, then perhaps it wasn't so surprising that he'd come to Dallas to see her, after all.

Jessica smiled at her image in the mirror. She was almost giddy with anticipation. That was a refreshing change. When she'd gone out on those blind dates, and with Tommy Jack Simons, she'd had trouble mustering up even a little enthusiasm.

She decided to wear the soft blue sleeveless silk dress she'd bought in May for her firm's twenty-fifth anniversary party. That evening had turned out to be an uncomfortable one. It had brought home that, as a young widow, she no longer fit in with the married crowd. Nor did hanging out with the singles seem quite right. But tonight with Wiley would be different.

Even as her excitement grew, Jessica had to caution

herself against putting too much stock in this date. Because Wiley was her uncle's friend, she trusted him, but she was also aware that she didn't really *know* the man. Not deep down. Sides of him could turn up that weren't all that attractive. It would be important to keep her expectations low.

No sooner had she made that resolution than she recalled the fun they'd had the night they'd dined at the Cowboy Club, and how flattered she'd felt when Wiley had shown up on her doorstep the previous evening. Of course, neither was a guarantee of how the future would play out. The real question was whether or not he'd have enough substance to interest her beyond a couple of meals and some conversation. But then, in asking that, she was probably getting ahead of herself. It was those darned expectations again. She simply had to keep them in check. Lord knew, there was nothing to be gained by putting pressure on either Wiley or her.

Jessica was arranging the last of the cheese on a serving plate she'd gotten as a wedding present when the doorbell rang. It was seven minutes after seven, perfect timing. Geoff had been late to everything, but, in his case, he was usually impolitely late. More than once they'd arrived at a dinner party after the salad course.

Jessica went to the door, pausing before the hall mirror for a last peek at herself. The rosy glow in her cheeks was natural. She shuddered to think she was blowing this completely out of proportion. But boy, for the moment at least, it sure felt good!

Pulling the door open, she was pleased to find Wiley looking suave and sophisticated in a dark suit and burgundy tie. No country boy, this guy. He could just as easily have occupied an executive suite in one of Dallas's high-rise office buildings. He was looking her over, too.

"You look beautiful," he said, his bluish-gray eyes twinkling.

As he said it, he pulled a bouquet of baby yellow roses from behind his back, presenting them to her in a gallant fashion. Jessica's glowing cheeks burned even hotter.

"Oh, how sweet. Thank you."

She was sniffing the flowers as Wiley closed the door, then slipped up close enough to kiss her on the cheek, his cologne smelling intoxicatingly manly. He looked as happy as she felt.

"Seems to me there's a song about Texas and yellow roses," he said.

"Guess I *am* a Texan now," she said, sniffing the roses again.

Wiley touched her arm. "Hopefully, not for long."

She smiled. "Are you going to give me a hard time about moving to Red Rock?" she asked playfully.

"Won't say a word about Colorado, if you don't want me to."

"I guess as long as it's a soft sell, I won't mind."

"I can make it just as soft as you like," he said with a wink.

She gave an audible sigh, liking the way he bantered with her. "I think I'll put these in water," she said, sniffing the roses again.

"Mind if I watch?" he asked. "I don't want to miss a moment of your company."

She nodded and led the way to the kitchen, thinking that Wiley Cooper was sure sounding suave for a cowboy.

As he stood at the doorway watching, she trimmed the stems of the roses and put them in a cut-glass vase that had belonged to her mother. Then she held them up for him to admire.

"Beautiful and beautiful," he said. "Flowers and flower girl both."

She wagged her finger at him. "I've got to keep my eye on you."

Wiley grinned, looking once again like the man she'd danced with at the Cowboy Club months earlier.

"So," she said, putting down the vase on the counter, "what can I offer you to drink?"

"What are you having?"

"I've got a bottle of Chardonnay chilling in the fridge. Unless a Merlot is more to your taste."

Wiley shrugged. "I won't pretend to know a lot about wines." He chuckled. "'A fraud can only hide for so long,' as my grandpappy Cyrus Cable used to say. 'Better you wear an honest face, even if it's modest.'"

"Your grandpappy sounds like a wise man."

"I like to think so. 'The difference between know-how and wisdom is doing.' That's another of his favorite sayings," Wiley added. "The man could talk, but he was also a doer."

"Might that describe you, as well?" she asked.

"Considering I've got the paper and the ranch, I guess I'm guilty of both a little saying and a little doing. Keeps life from getting boring."

"I don't think there are boring lives," she said thoughtfully, "only boring people."

"You've got a point."

She snatched the Chardonnay from the fridge and the corkscrew from the utensil drawer. Wiley took them from her hands. She retrieved a couple of wineglasses while he uncorked the bottle. After he poured, they each took a glass.

"To new beginnings," he said.

"New beginnings."

They looked into each other's eyes as they sipped their wine. Jessica thought of something her mother had said to her about men when she was a teenager and they were still living in Colorado—"When kissing a cowboy in the rain, make sure he has a big enough hat for you both to stay dry." All Jessica could say was it sure as heck had been raining on her for a long time now, and Wiley Cooper's hat was the first she'd seen that looked big enough to crawl under.

WILEY FOLLOWED HER into the front room, liking the way her dress shimmered as she moved. Jessica was graceful—he'd noticed how fluid her movements were even before they'd had their first dance at the Cowboy Club.

Jessica set the plate with cheese and crackers on the coffee table. She sat down on the pale yellow couch and Wiley sat next to her, not quite as close as he'd have liked, but close enough to take in the lilac scent of her perfume. She took a sip of wine, obviously contemplating him, before she spoke. "Uncle Ford told me you have a grown daughter. Do you see her much?"

Wiley blinked. The last thing he'd expected her to ask about was his child. Hell, he had no reason to think she'd even *know* about Lindsay.

"Maybe that's too personal a question," she said before he had a chance to answer. "Sorry if I brought up something I shouldn't have."

He hesitated, picking his words carefully. "It's a sensitive subject, but not too personal a question. Besides, it's part of who I am." He told her about how Joyce intentionally got pregnant, then went off with the baby and remarried.

"The woman sounds horrible, but the worst was depriving you of your child. That was awful."

"In retrospect, I'd have to agree with you, but at the time I was relieved. Of course, I was awfully young and stupid, too. Once I convinced myself that Lindsay was in a happy home and well provided for, I decided it was in everyone's interest for me to let go."

"So you never see her?"

Wiley shook his head. "She doesn't even know I exist."

"That must be hard for you."

"I try not to dwell on it. As long as she's happy, I tell myself that's good enough for me."

There was an awkward silence during which they each sipped their wine. Wiley had a bite from the cheese tray.

"Have you wanted other children?" she asked tentatively.

Again, he shook his head. "To be perfectly honest, I haven't even wanted a wife. My friends say I'm snake bit." He shrugged. "I say I'm cautious."

"I see. Well, in principle, how do you feel about having a family?"

He looked into her beautiful blue eyes, wondering why she was pushing so hard. Probably because the subject tormented her, he decided. "I'm coming up on my fortieth birthday soon. That's not too old to have kids, I know, but it's not something I've been counting on, either." He paused to take a deep breath. "How about you? You're still a young woman. Do you want another child?"

He watched as she seemed to stiffen. "We seem to have gotten right to the heart of the matter, haven't we?"

"I'm sorry. I shouldn't have—"

"No, I'm the one who brought it up." She turned the stem of the wineglass in her hand. "Having lost my daughter, I know pain. It's something I never wish to experience again." She lowered her head, but not before he saw the tears forming in her eyes. "The thought of having another baby and risking losing it is…well, more than I can handle."

He reached over and took her hand. "Maybe we should talk about something else."

She looked up at him earnestly. "I guess I wanted you to know how I felt right up front. That's presumptuous of me, maybe, and I truly don't mean anything by it…except that I want to be really clear about the way I feel. I promised myself if I ever saw a man more than once, I'd let him know where I stand. There's no point in unnecessary surprises."

"I appreciate that, Jessica. I really do."

She wiped away a tear that had slipped over her lid. "Guess you could say that, unlike you, I *am* snake bit, although I find myself wanting to tell people I'm not what I appear."

"You *are* what you appear. You've lived through tragedy, you've been wounded, but you're not alone, not the only one who's endured this kind of pain. In some small way, perhaps, that's a comfort to you. I know it's a comfort to me."

She nodded but didn't speak. And as he watched the evening light play across her pretty face, he reflected that, deep down, they were very alike. They both had suffered losses and been hurt. But now, having met Jessica, he was ready to move on, to give love a chance. The real question was, did she feel the same?

## 4

JESSICA WAS NERVOUS about dining at Nero's until she recalled Wiley's toast to "a new beginning." That's what this was, a new beginning. For both of them. Even so, her heart was tripping as they pulled up in front of the restaurant, which was located in an older building on Lower Greenville.

There was a canopy extending from the door to the curb. Wiley took the receipt from the parking attendant and they went to the door and stepped inside. The decor was Italian, the colors mostly red and black. The twin-paned windows in front were draped. To the right was a long bar, with tables in the middle of the room and booths on the left. The place glowed with candlelight.

They were seated in a booth. Wiley looked pleased and proud, very much as Geoff had when they'd come to celebrate her pregnancy. Her life had been so full of hope and promise that night. In a thousand years she would never have guessed that a mere three years later she'd be a widow and childless.

She glanced at Wiley again. He was unaware of her angst, which should have pleased her. Oddly, she found that she almost resented him. That wasn't fair. It was her fault they had come here. Lord knew, he'd told her where they were going and she could easily have asked him to change their reservation. The plain fact was, there were associations everywhere and it was no one's fault. It was up to her to put that chapter of her life behind her and move on. "New beginnings, new beginnings, new beginnings," she said to herself, over and over.

Wiley picked up the wine card, asking if she cared for a glass with dinner.

Jessica was going to say she didn't really want any wine, but then realized she did. The night she'd come with Geoff, she hadn't drunk because she was expecting. Now she had absolutely no reason not to enjoy herself. Besides, if she truly wanted to change her attitude, she ought to begin by taking advantage of this new situation. "Yes, thank you."

"Another Chardonnay?"

"That would be nice."

Wiley had the waiter bring the wine while they studied the menus.

"You won't find food like this in Red Rock, I'll have to concede that," he said amiably.

"I enjoyed our dinner at the Cowboy Club," she said, wishing that's where they were right now—anywhere but here amid all the memories of her pregnancy.

Wiley noticed the hitch in her voice.

Jessica, catching his look, forced a smile. "What are you going to have?" she asked quickly to cover her true feelings.

"I don't know. Everything looks so good." He perused the menu for another moment or two. "Do you have a recommendation? You have eaten here before, haven't you? I didn't ask."

Jessica swallowed hard. "Yes, I have."

Wiley didn't ignore her reaction this time. "Jessica?"

She turned her head, biting her lip hard, hating her sadness, the pain that seemed to come upon her no matter what she did.

"Are you all right?"

"I'm afraid this place has some associations," she said, barely managing a whisper. She told him the story.

"You should have said something," he told her, looking pained. "We don't have to stay."

"No, I can't spend my life afraid to go places, afraid to remember."

He nodded sympathetically. "My grandpappy Cyrus warned that life was like juggling pitchforks sometimes."

"He was right."

"And he also said that life is simpler when you plow around the stumps."

Jessica gave him a wry smile. "Meaning I should move to Red Rock, I suppose?"

Wiley shrugged. "Not too many stumps out there. Plenty of red rocks, big open sky and friendly people, though."

"And you."

"And me." He took her hand, pulled it to his mouth and kissed her fingers. "Are you all right? *Really* all right?"

She nodded.

"Good, then let's decide what we want to eat. Might as well go for broke because if you come to Red Rock, it'll be steak and buffalo stew and armadillo eggs and snake-bites."

Jessica appreciated the way he'd managed to turn her mood around. Maybe the secret was to acknowledge her feelings. Or maybe it was that she needed someone like Wiley, who could empathize.

She relaxed after that, and by the time their meals came she was beginning to feel almost mellow. Since Wiley was driving, he only had one glass. But, for once, Jessica felt free to let go. She'd never been able to do that around Geoff because he often drank too much and she'd felt that one of them had to be responsible. But Jessica felt she could put herself in Wiley's hands and still be safe. That was a vote of confidence, considering how briefly she'd known him. While they were having their coffee, she told him how comfortable he made her feel.

"If I had to pick an effect I had on a woman, that wouldn't be a bad choice."

Jessica reached over and put her hand on his. "That's not all I feel, of course. But it's all I'm willing to admit to…at least at this early stage."

Wiley seemed to like that. He toyed with her fingers, looking again as if he wanted to kiss her. She wished he would.

"Do you like to walk?" she asked.

"You mean hike, backpack?"

"No, just walk, stroll." Then she chuckled. "Come to think of it, that's a silly question to ask a cowboy. You ride everywhere, don't you? Either on horseback or in your pickup."

"Mostly, but I'm not averse to a stroll in the moonlight."

"How did you know that's what I was thinking?"

Wiley smiled. "Maybe by the glow on your cheeks."

Jessica felt herself blush even more. "All right, cowboy. I was thinking of taking you to this pretty lake. It's nearby, in a nice residential area. A good place for a stroll."

He beamed at her. "Why are we waiting?"

Wiley called for the check. Jessica was happy to skip dessert. She'd eaten more than in any two normal days. She told him her doctor wanted her to eat more. "You look like you could use a little fattening up," he said.

"You think I'm too thin?"

"Hard to criticize anything I see when I look at you," he said.

She gave him an admonishing look. "Come on, let me show you Whiterock Lake."

FROM GREENVILLE they took Mockingbird Lane to the lake. The jogging path around the lake made a pleasant place to stroll. The moon shone so bright they could see the silvery green of the surrounding lawns and trees. The night air was lulling, softer than it had been earlier. Jessica took his arm.

"This has been a wonderful evening," she said. "I hope it hasn't been too tedious for you. I was kind of emotional for a minute, back in the restaurant."

"Don't worry about it. Your feelings are your feelings. And, to tell you the truth, I can't think of an evening I've enjoyed more."

"You have a knack for making a lady feel awfully special, Wiley Cooper. I can't believe one of those Red Rock gals hasn't snagged you long before now. Do you have a dark side you hide well?"

He grinned. "Ah, now you want me to get myself in trouble, is that it, Counselor?"

"No, it's a serious question."

"Well…let me see. I'm stubborn and sometimes a little single-minded."

"That can be either good or bad."

"Yeah," he chuckled, "depending which side of the issue you're on."

"What else?"

"I tend to be suspicious of people's motives."

"Funny," she said, "that doesn't sound at all like you."

"Oh, I make an exception for lovely ladies. But the newspaper man in me makes me always doubt, look beneath the surface of things."

They strolled for a while. The caress of the breeze and the fragrance in the air made her even more aware of his masculinity and appeal.

"So, how about you?" Wiley said. "Turnabout's fair play. What are your faults?"

"That's easy. I'm pessimistic and not very trusting."

"Have you always been that way, or just since your loss?"

The way he went right to the heart of the issue startled her, though it shouldn't have because he'd been so direct earlier. "You're right. I've lost a lot of people I love and it's changed me."

"I'd say you're entitled," he said, putting his hand over the one holding his arm.

"You're a sweet man."

"And the pessimism's got to be due to circumstance. Below the surface, I bet you're a hopeful, positive person."

"How do you know?"

"I just do. You wouldn't be fighting so hard if that wasn't true."

Jessica smiled to herself, thinking he was right. Wiley was the kind of man who could see beneath her pain and defenses, who could help her become the best person she could be. That was comforting, though it was scary, too, because she was almost afraid to hope again. She couldn't face the pain of another disappointment.

She looked out across the placid water of the small lake. The glassy surface reflected the moonlight.

"On a Saturday afternoon, there are lots of little sailboats and canoes out there," she told him. "Geoff and I used to bring Cassandra down here in her stroller."

"Does it make you sad to be here?" he asked, his voice low, even.

"No, it's different at night." She turned to him. "This is the first time I've walked by the lake in the moonlight. In a way, I suppose, I'm sharing something from my past, but I'm doing it in a new way. I feel good about that—both that I can do it, and that I'm doing it with you."

She watched the moonlight play across his face, throwing it into sharp relief as she spoke. He looked very handsome, but also thoughtful. Then the corner of his mouth bent into a smile.

"I feel pretty good about this evening myself, Jessica. And I want you to know, it's all because of you."

His words sent a surge of joy through her. She glanced toward the water, seeing a large weeping willow at the water's edge. "Come on," she said, taking his hand and leading him toward the tree.

They ducked under the branches and into the dark protection of the weeping willow's boughs, lacy moonbeams filtering through the leaves. There was enough illumination for them to make out the contours of each other's bodies. Jessica reached up and tentatively touched Wiley's cheek. He moved his head to give her palm a quick kiss.

The caress was so sweet that she was filled with longing. This was one of those rare moments she would remember always, she was certain—like the first time she'd been kissed and the first time she'd made love. Jessica closed her eyes and tried to imprint the moment in her mind. The moonlight reflecting on the lake. The soft hush of air coming off the water. And Wiley, kissing the palm of her hand.

It was lushly romantic. But not because of the setting. Or her mood. She felt this way because Wiley was a kindred spirit. He understood her suffering and her loneliness because he'd suffered and he'd been lonely, too.

"I'd like to be privy to some of those thoughts that just passed through your mind," he said in a low voice.

She sighed. "I was thinking about the past."

"Not unhappy memories, I hope."

She shook her head. "No. I'm actually just savoring the moment. Making a new memory."

"I like the sound of that."

"So do I." She gave his cheek a final caress and turned

toward the water. Wiley was so close to her that she could feel the heat of his body.

His hand brushed aside the hair at the nape of her neck and he kissed her, just behind the ear. Jessica shivered with desire, wanting more yet afraid to move for fear the magic of the moment would vanish.

"You know," he whispered, "this is the first time I've ever kissed a woman under a willow tree."

With that, she turned into his embrace and he kissed her deeply. Jessica felt her desire break free with a rush. Months of repression and emotional isolation spilled out of her. Her body tingled and warmed in his embrace. Wiley crushed her close to him, his fingers digging through the fabric of her dress and into her flesh.

Her heart beat wildly, not letting up even after the kiss ended. She pressed her face against his neck, feeling his heat against her already burning cheeks. They were both breathing hard. Wiley ran his hand down her bare arm, making her skin feel more alive wherever he touched her.

She closed her eyes, remembering the first time she'd made love. She'd been so nervous, afraid to let it happen yet wanting to know the unknown. In the end she had been disappointed. What would that time have been like if Wiley had been her lover? She tried to imagine it, but instead of seeing herself as a nervous eighteen-year-old, she thought of herself as she was now—a woman who knew what she wanted and how she wanted it.

That scared her. It was way too soon for her to feel that way. Wasn't it?

There was a whoop of glee then from the pathway beyond the willow. Jessica opened her eyes in time to see two teens speed by on in-line skates.

"Perhaps we should go," Wiley said.

She nodded.

He pushed aside the drooping boughs and, taking her

hand, led her back toward the path. In a way, the spell was broken. But in another way, it wasn't. Jessica knew that she still wanted him. She longed to be in his arms again, to have him kiss her one more time. And she couldn't help wondering if he felt the same.

They said very little during the drive back to Richardson. When they came to a stop sign, Jessica reached out and touched his knee, wanting to make contact with him. Wiley took her hand and kissed it, then resumed driving.

She studied him. The angular good looks of his face were thrown into relief by the moonlight and the occasional streetlights. She thought of how hard and lean the muscles of his body had felt against hers when he'd held her in his arms under the willow.

Her strong feeling of desire surprised her—not just its sudden appearance, but also its intensity. Surely it wasn't that she'd been deprived for so long. The thought of sex hardly entered her mind anymore. She'd even wondered if she'd lost the desire for good. But Wiley Cooper proved she hadn't. He made her feel womanly and alive.

They stopped in front of her house, locked the car and went together to the front door. Her fingers shook as she tried to put the key in the lock. Wiley took her hand, steadying it, helping her to insert the key.

There was odd power in that, but she said nothing. She started to turn on the light in the entry hall, but didn't. There was plenty of ambient light streaming in through the front bay window.

"Would you like some wine?" she asked softly.

"No," he said.

"Mind if I have some?"

"Not at all."

Jessica went to the kitchen where the bottle of Chardonnay was still sitting on the counter. She'd forgotten to put it in the refrigerator when they'd left, but it didn't matter. She half filled the wineglass next to it, not knowing whether it had been his or hers, not caring. She took a couple of hasty sips before turning. Wiley was standing at the door, exactly where he'd been when she arranged the flowers.

"This has been a wonderful evening, Jessica. Very special."

She took another sip of wine and then set down her glass. "Yes. For me, too."

"Is that true?"

She opened her lips to speak, but no words came out. How could she explain what being with him this evening had meant? All the memories, the conflicting feelings. Could he possibly understand the desire, the pent-up longing? Or how she was struggling to put it all into perspective?

Suddenly, all the emotions she'd felt that evening crowded in on her. She burst into tears. Wiley instantly came to her side, pulling her into his arms. He held her close, gently rubbing her back as she wept.

"Tell me what I can do to help. What's wrong?"

"I...I'm afraid."

He kissed her hair. "Of me?"

Jessica looked up at him, her eyes blurry with tears. "No. Of myself. Of the way I feel."

"I don't want you to be afraid," he said softly. "Not of me. And certainly not of the way you feel. Ever."

His words made her smile. They were so liberating, so accepting. And because of that, she felt free—freer than she'd felt in a long time. Free to tell him what she wanted.

"I like it when you hold me like this," she said.

He chuckled. "And I like holding you." He pulled back to look at her. "Almost as much as I liked kissing you."

"I liked kissing you, too. Very much."

Wiley didn't need more of an invitation. He kissed her hard on the mouth. She wound her arms around his neck, pulling his head close to hers. As before, she felt the heat of desire. She parted her lips and let his tongue slip into her mouth. She felt so connected to him, and yet at the same time, not connected enough. She wanted more.

When he finally pulled away, she trembled and looked up into his dark face. It seemed even more sexy for its unfamiliarity. She felt another pang of longing as he trailed his fingertips down her neck.

"Perhaps I should go now," he said.

"No," she said, shaking her head. "Please don't."

"I think it's best."

"I don't want you to leave," she said firmly.

Wiley froze with uncertainty. Reaching up, she pulled his face down and made him kiss her again. Instantly, her heat fed his and they were kissing with a fervor that left Jessica breathless. Thoughts started to gather in her mind only to dissipate, like fog in the sunlight. There was only need. Desire and fulfillment. Her desire and the fulfillment she found in Wiley Cooper's arms.

She was barely aware of it as he scooped her into his arms and carried her to the spare bedroom. Briefly, the thought passed through her mind that she was glad they were not going to be in her marital bed. But even that concern vanished as Wiley unzipped her dress and helped her out of it. There was no rational thought. There was only her need—to be a woman again.

When she was naked, Jessica felt a sudden rush of modesty. Embarrassed, she slipped under the covers of the bed. When she looked up, she saw that Wiley was stripping away his clothing. She watched transfixed as he revealed more and more of himself.

When he was totally naked, the size and strength of his masculine body seemed at once overwhelming and reassuring. He slipped under the sheet and laid his arm across her chest, pressing his face to her neck and inhaling her scent. Jessica felt the heat of his body, her insides growing creamy with desire. Wiley drew a line of feather kisses along her shoulder and collarbone. She was afraid, but at the same time, on fire.

He drew back and looked into her eyes. "Are you protected?" he asked, caressing her cheek with one finger. She assured him that she was, and he continued his sensual ministrations.

This lover who had come to her uninvited and out of nowhere was gentle, yet strong. He did not rush her, allowing time for the heat of desire to overwhelm her. In the darkness and with her eyes closed, she could barely picture Wiley's face, yet his spirit was as strong as the fingers arousing her flesh. How could his touch feel so natural and right when she was so unsure? And why was it so important to her that she give herself to him?

Reaching down, she found him erect. He groaned at her touch. The heat coming from his body was searing, but she wanted it. She wanted life to be pumped back into her. She wanted once again to care, to feel, to live.

"Please make love to me," she murmured. "Please."

With the touch of his fingers, Wiley caressed her center, stroking her until she thought she might come. When she felt herself on the hard edge of desire, she stopped him and pulled him on top of her.

He entered her then, large, hard and overpowering. At first he was gentle, holding back his force until she was in her fullest throw of pleasure. He changed his pace then, going a little deeper with each thrust, moving a little faster, until she knew they wouldn't be able to hold off much longer.

They came together. Afterward they lay in each other's arms, breathing heavily, their hearts raging, the scent of their bodies filling their lungs. Wiley rolled off her, but he held her hand, entwining his fingers in hers.

He kissed the palm of her hand. "Jessica, I'm going to break my promise. I'm going to ask you to move to Red Rock."

Thoughts of that possibility hadn't entered her mind for hours, but there was no question it was the most vital issue between them. The prospect was inviting. But common sense told her to be cautious.

"We've got to be careful not to make too much of this," she said. "No matter how beautiful it was."

"I know. I'm only asking that you come to Red Rock. I'm not asking for a commitment of any sort."

She took his hand and pressed it to her cheek as she looked into his shadowed eyes. "That's easier said than done. There are always...expectations."

"Perhaps. But I've been alone long enough to know that I'd rather have expectations of something wonderful happening than to have no expectations at all."

## 5

SALLY ANNE SAT on the bench of the bus stop in front of the Conoco station and waited, just as Jason had told her. Nathaniel was asleep in his basket next to her, his blanket draped over the top to protect him from the late-morning sun. She stared up the street, on the lookout for a red semi-truck, anguishing.

She had discovered that making the decision to give up her baby and actually doing it were two different things. When Jason had finally gotten back from his road trip, and she'd told him what she had decided to do about the baby, he'd shrugged and said, "Fine."

"Fine?" she'd said tearfully. "Is that all?"

"What do you expect me to say?"

"Jason, he's your baby, too!"

Jason had looked annoyed then and said, "I gave you a thousand bucks, Sally Anne, everything I had in my savings account. You didn't have to have the baby. You *wanted* to have him. I told you you were on your own. What do you expect from me now?"

"Maybe a little help getting Nathaniel to Red Rock."

"Can't you take a bus or something?"

She could have killed him, he was so heartless. She'd long since given up any hope of Jason playing a meaningful role in either Nathaniel's or her life, but it seemed the least he could do was help her solve the problem of getting their baby into a happy home.

"I haven't wanted to say anything, Jason, but I could make a lot of trouble for you. You might not have much money, but I don't even have a regular job. We wouldn't even have anything to eat if I didn't work at the Food-Mart. And you know what would happen if I went to the welfare office. They'd have you paying child support in a flash."

"So what do you want me to do?" he'd asked sullenly. "Drive you there?"

"Would you?"

"I can't just up and take a truck to Red Rock. My routes are all east nowadays."

"There must be some way," she'd said.

Then Jason told her he had a buddy, an independent trucker who had contracts to service accounts in Albuquerque and Phoenix. "Maybe the next time he does a run that way, he could give you a lift."

"So how do I get back?"

"Maybe you shouldn't come back," Jason had said. "There's lots of jobs in a place like Phoenix. What's here for you?"

At first, Sally Anne was angry and hurt. But the more she thought about it, the more she realized Jason was right. Providing for Nathaniel was only the first step—she had to support herself, as well. She needed a job, a life. In Phoenix, she could start over.

Jason told her he'd need time to arrange things. Naturally, they wouldn't be able to tell his friend they were abandoning the baby. They agreed to say she was leaving the baby with relatives for a while. They made their deal, but she explained that she couldn't hold out much longer. It was tough emotionally and financially. Jason gave her sixty dollars, and two weeks later he gave her another seventy. Last night, when he'd come by to tell her that his friend Monty would be at the Conoco station at eleven, he gave her two hundred dollars. "You'll need it when you get to Phoenix," he'd said.

Sally Anne had given him a hug, which she could tell

made Jason uncomfortable. She knew he didn't really care about her, much less the baby. "Don't you want to say goodbye to your son?" she'd asked.

Jason had hung his head. "Why bother? Never going to see him again."

Sally Anne figured Jason wasn't as heartless as he seemed. He was scared, and he was running from his feelings.

Now she looked back over her shoulder at the clock on the service-station wall. It was ten after eleven and still no sign of Monty in his red semi. What if he didn't show up? She'd already given up her room and wouldn't likely get it back, even with cash in hand. She and Nathaniel had been a problem for their landlady, Mrs. Gibbs. Sally Anne was lucky the woman hadn't gone to the police. "I know you belong someplace and are hiding," Mrs. Gibbs had said, "and I don't like it." Fortunately, though, she'd taken the rent money and looked the other way.

Nathaniel stirred in his basket and Sally Anne looked down at him, allowing herself to feel her sorrow. The past few weeks she'd tried not to think about it, tried to concentrate on her hopes for a better life for her baby, not her love for him. In Phoenix, she would start over, maybe with a new name. One day, maybe, she'd marry and have other children, but not until she was ready and could give her family a home.

The baby gave a small cry, crunching up his face and opening his eyes. Sally Anne resisted the temptation to touch his cheek. The past few weeks she'd touched him as little as possible. Soon Nathaniel would be getting his love from someone else. The time had come to let go.

Just then a big red semi-truck pulled up to the curb, stopping right in front of her. The driver leaned across and opened the passenger door.

"Hi," he called. "You Sally Anne?"

"Yes," she said, getting up.

"I'm Monty. Hop in."

Sally Anne shoved her small suitcase in the cab first, then Nathaniel in his basket. Finally, she climbed aboard. Monty was chubby and about Jason's age. He had a friendly face and an outgoing manner. He also had on a wedding ring. She was glad.

"You want to go to Red Rock, then Phoenix, right?"

"Right," she said.

"It's a good idea to make sure you and the bus are going to the same place," he said with a laugh. Monty put the big truck in gear, checked his rearview mirror, and the vehicle lumbered into motion. "Picked up a guy at a truck stop in Wyoming once who said he was headed to Portland, same place I was going. He promptly fell asleep and when we got to Salt Lake we discovered he was headed to Portland, Maine, and I was headed to Portland, Oregon."

"The Red Rock I'm headed for is in western Colorado."

"Bingo!" Monty said. He laughed and took a candy bar from his pocket. "Want half?"

Sally Anne shook her head. "No, thanks."

Monty had gone through the shifting cycle and the truck was rolling smoothly down the highway. Sally Anne looked out the window, knowing a chapter of her life was coming to a close. She wouldn't be free, though, until Nathaniel was in safe hands. Her baby's future was in Red Rock. The ride there would be the longest of her life.

WILEY SUBTLY CHECKED his watch, then leaned back in his chair. He and his friends were in the back room at the Cowboy Club, playing their usual game of Thursday-night poker. Though he'd dropped out of the current hand before the draw, he was doing well—better than usual—but poker was hardly foremost in his thoughts. After six weeks, the day of Jessica's arrival had finally come and he couldn't wait to see her.

Ford, of course, knew that Jessica would be arriving that evening. In fact, Jessica's uncle had asked her to meet him at the Cowboy Club so he could hand over the keys to the house he'd rented for her. But no one else in town knew about her coming, or that Wiley had gone to Dallas to see her.

Wiley knew that Ford suspected he and Jessica had feelings for each other, but the lawyer didn't know what had transpired in Dallas. Once he'd gotten home, Wiley could hardly believe what had happened himself.

"I'm not one to pry," Ford had said a month earlier when he'd called Wiley with news that Jessica was moving to Red Rock, "but whatever you said or did down there sure as the dickens turned the girl's head. I know the prospect of joining my practice wasn't what tipped the scales."

As a gentleman, Wiley had to let Ford wonder, but the old pettifogger was no fool. He knew romance was in the air. Wiley had left him to speculate, only saying, "I encouraged her to look at the big picture—social, as well as professional."

Ford had given him a quirky smile. "As her uncle and closest relative, I thank you, Wiley."

Quentin Starr, having won the hand they'd been playing, raked in his chips. Heath Barnett, the big loser of the evening, got to his feet and stretched.

"Maybe something to eat will change my luck," he said. "Did you say some sandwiches were on their way, Dax?"

"Wanda should be coming through that door any minute," Dax Charboneau replied.

"Maybe we should take a break," Ford said.

Everybody agreed that would be a good idea.

The group met every week at the Cowboy Club, not only because it was the premier watering hole and restaurant in town, but for other reasons, as well. There was something special about the place—a mood, a feeling of romance with a capital *R*, that couldn't be denied. Pretty near everyone who'd ever been to the place felt it.

In the center of the room where they played poker, there was a big round oak table. The walls were decorated with pictures of movie stars who had come to Red Rock to film westerns way back in the forties, fifties and sixties. Photographs of John Wayne, Jimmy Stewart, Glenn Ford, Maureen O'Hara, Virginia Mayo and Errol Flynn graced the walls, along with pictures of Julia Sommers and Cody James, who had jointly owned the Cowboy Club until Dax Charboneau had bought out Julia. Cody had died the year before.

Wiley checked his watch again. Ford noticed, giving him a knowing smile.

Wiley and Ford had eaten in the dining room before the game began. With a buffalo steak under his belt, and a fat slab of apple pie and vanilla ice cream for dessert, Wiley wasn't hungry. He wouldn't have thought Ford would be either, but he had mumbled something about a ham sandwich sounding good.

Over dinner, they'd talked about Jessica's impending arrival. "I can see you're even more eager to see her than I am," Ford had said.

"That obvious, is it?"

"Son, you have the look of a man in love."

Wiley had only grinned, which probably said it all.

Things had been going well, it was true, though there'd been a few minor bumps along the way. Wiley had learned of Jessica's decision to move to Red Rock even before Ford. She'd called him the night before she'd given her uncle the official word.

"I've put a lot of thought into it, Wiley," she'd said.

"I'm very fond of you, as you know, but I think we need an understanding."

"What sort of understanding, Counselor?"

"First, I don't think either of us should feel an obligation. The two nights you were here with me were among the happiest and most enjoyable I've ever spent with a man. But that in itself can't be the reason for me moving to Red Rock."

"Maybe not *the* reason, but it can be *a* reason, can't it?"

"Of course, and I admit it's a factor," she'd said. "But we may or may not have a future with each other. What I'm saying is, there shouldn't be expectations."

"I don't feel you owe me anything, if that's what you're worried about," he'd told her. "We have a friendship. If something more permanent comes of it, fine. No pressure, no expectations."

"I'm glad you feel that way," she'd said, sounding relieved.

"But I think it's safe to say I've got my eye on you, sweetheart. I won't put the Double C brand on your backside quite yet, though. You might enjoy keeping company with me once you arrive in Red Rock, or you just might find yourself a better deal."

"That's not the issue, Wiley."

"Point is, you're free to do as you wish, and what's transpired between us is our secret."

"I remember small-town life well enough to know it has its complications."

"Well, no matter what, I *am* looking forward to seeing you," he'd told her. "And whatever the future brings, I have fond memories of our time together, too."

Jessica had seemed content with that, and he was relieved he'd told her what she wanted to hear. In spite of his words to the contrary, as far as he was concerned, he *had* put his brand on her. The lady didn't know it yet, and he might have to hold back for a while, but in the end, he intended to have her.

It had been six weeks since he'd seen her, though they'd talked three or four times a week, discussing anything and everything under the sun. Just talking to her made him feel terrific. Not only was it enjoyable, it was increasingly more comfortable. And to Wiley, it was damn encouraging.

Once Jessica had made her decision to come to Colorado, she had a lot of work to do in preparation for the move. Wiley'd considered offering to fly down to give her a hand, but he was afraid that might have added to the pressure. So, instead, he'd played it cool, letting things happen in their own good time. That was difficult enough, but the hardest part was pretending to the world that nothing had happened.

Dax, his best friend in town, was sitting directly across from him now. Wiley watched as his buddy manipulated the cards with magician-like dexterity. "You've been awfully quiet tonight, partner," Dax said to him. "You've got something big going on at the paper?"

"Nothing special," Wiley replied. "I've just got the usual balls in the air, trying to make sure I don't drop any."

"I've got a few things on the go, too," Quentin said, "but no two things as diverse as ranching and running a newspaper. Don't know how you switch gears."

Heath, who was mostly taciturn, spoke up unexpectedly. "Wiley doesn't have a steady woman keepin' the collar on him. That makes it easier to get a lot done."

"What are you saying, Heath, that when a fella gets married, he becomes half a man?" Dax said.

"No, but his time gets taken up by domestic matters."

"Chloe does keep me busy," Dax admitted. "But not at the expense of my business. And, as you can see, I still find time for a night out with you boys."

"How long do you think Chloe'll tolerate your poker nights?" Ford chided. "I've been around longer than the rest of you and I've seen the married ones disappear one by one...once the honeymoon's over."

The others laughed. Dax grinned coolly. Because of his card-playing prowess and his black clothes, he was widely regarded as a riverboat gambler in the true sense of the word, but there was little doubt his new wife had changed him.

"You know what the real problem is?" Dax said. "You boys don't like me taking home your hard-earned money, that's all."

It was only fitting that they'd give Dax a hard time, considering this was his first poker night since his wedding. He and Chloe had honeymooned in New Orleans, then had been busy finding a house to rent, moving in and getting settled. Since Chloe had relocated her shoe-design company from New York to Red Rock, moving her business into the old saddlery at the same time, the project had been a huge undertaking. Everyone liked her and there wasn't a soul who didn't think she was good for Dax.

Wanda, the hostess of the Cowboy Club and practically an institution in her own right, arrived then with another huge tray of sandwiches, breezing into the room. Wanda had big white hair and wore false eyelashes. She was a middle-aged widow, warm and friendly and a little overweight. Tonight she was wearing her usual big multicolored Mexican skirt with a white off-the-shoulder blouse.

As she began passing out the sandwiches, she spoke to Ford. "I got a call from your niece ten minutes ago, Mr. Mayor."

Wiley's ears perked up.

"She had car trouble," Wanda went on. "Had to be towed into La Mesa. Upshot is, it was already so late she decided to grab a bite there. She said she ought to be here in the next hour."

"Your niece decide to move up here, after all?" Quentin asked. "Last I heard she hadn't made up her mind."

"She's making the move, all right," Ford replied. "Which means my life is about to get a little bit easier. Good thing, too, with the election coming up."

Wiley had noticed the interest in Quentin's voice, and he didn't like it. At six-five, Quentin was the tallest man in the room, though they were all over six feet, except for Ford. Quentin had thick browny-blond hair, was in his mid-thirties, about the same age as Dax and Heath. Quentin had been a local boy—a "bad-boy" local boy, by most folk's reckoning—who'd gone to Texas to make a fortune. He'd recently returned to Red Rock, bought Dax's house and darn near all his furniture with it, and then had invested in Julia Sommers's ghost-town project.

Like the others, except for Dax, Quentin was a bachelor. He'd undoubtedly heard how attractive Jessica was from all the talk around town. In a place where the number of attractive, available women was limited, the arrival of a new prospect always made single men sit up and take note.

"I have a hunch you'll have to arm-wrestle Wiley for her," Dax said, taking the opportunity to stir things up a little.

Quentin took a bite of sandwich. "Already staked a claim, have you, Wiley?"

Wiley clenched his teeth, but when he answered, his tone was nonchalant. "Let's just say Jessica and I are friends."

There were smiles all around the table. "No wonder you've been so quiet tonight," Quentin said.

Wanda had gone around the table, filling everybody's glass with beer. "You boys need anything else? Chips, snakebites, armadillo eggs? Bob needs to know 'cause he's getting ready to shut down the kitchen. The dining room emptied out half an hour ago."

Dax looked at each of them in turn. When nobody said anything, he told Wanda that they were fine. Wiley was the only one who hadn't taken a sandwich. Dax glanced around the table. "Everyone happy?"

They all nodded except for Heath. He pushed his straight brown hair off his forehead, grimacing.

"What do you need?" Dax asked him.

"Better cards."

Quentin shook his head. "Heath, you made enough money on that cattle-futures deal you and Dax had to buy half the town. So why are you complaining about a friendly game of poker?"

Heath scratched his ear and sighed. "Because my cards are lousy."

Ford chuckled. "He's got you there, son. As old Cyrus would have said, 'You can't blame a worm for not wantin' to go fishin'.'"

"I've got enough change in my pocket for a couple more hands," Heath said, "then I'm out of here." He dealt.

The room grew silent as the men waited for their cards. When Wiley picked up his hand, he saw he'd been dealt a full house. He had the bet and put in two five-dollar chips, figuring he might as well flush out the faint of heart. Ford immediately folded, so did Heath. Quentin and Dax stayed in. Heath asked Wiley how many cards he wanted. When he stood pat, several brows raised.

Quentin scrutinized him, obviously trying to decide if Wiley was bluffing. Strangely, Dax seemed to be off in a daze. Wiley started the betting. Quentin, a good poker player, folded. That left Dax, who toyed with his chips a moment or two, then saw Wiley's bet and raised him twenty.

Perspiration formed on his forehead but he decided to

see Dax's raise. He bumped him another ten. Dax raised another twenty. Wiley figured Dax had the better hand, but he couldn't fold now, not without seeing his friend's hand. "Okay, partner," he said. "Here's your twenty. What have you got?"

"Flush," Dax said, turning over his cards. "Spades."

Wiley grinned, sighing with relief. "For once, I beat you, amigo. Full boat."

Dax glanced down at the cards, his expression unchanging. "Congratulations, Wiley," he said. "Must be a good omen."

Wiley raked in his winnings. "Well, I think it's only fair that I be lucky at cards since you've been so lucky in love, marrying Chloe and all."

Dax chuckled. "A whole lot luckier that you might imagine. In fact, I have some good news."

The others looked Dax's way. He regarded each of them, smiling broadly. Then, after letting the drama build, he said, "Chloe and I are going to have a baby."

Eyebrows went up all around.

"This soon?" Heath said, then flushed.

Dax gave him a bemused look. "The honeymoon was quite successful...a little more so than we'd planned, but I'm thrilled and Chloe's in seventh heaven. She's been designing baby booties ever since she found out."

Ford slapped Dax on the back. "Good work. And congratulations to the both of you. You'll be great parents."

Dax shook his head. "Lord knows, we hope so. Chloe was an only child, you know, and with me being an orphan, we don't have much experience. But when she called her parents to tell them the news, they said they'd move here and be on hand to help us out any way they could."

"That'll be nice for Chloe," Quentin said.

"Me, too," Dax said. "They're good people. The only problem I see is finding places for everyone to live. That

Victorian we rented that used to belong to Doc Jasper won't really work for a family. We'll need to start building our new house right away. And we'll have to find a rental for my in-laws, too." Dax turned to Ford. "Do you know if Cody's house has been let? It might work for Chloe's parents, at least on an interim basis."

Ford shook his head. "Sorry, Dax, my niece beat you to the punch. Jessica's going to rent it until her place sells in Dallas."

"This move must be permanent," Quentin said. He glanced at Wiley. "Sounds like you might have impressed her as much as she impressed you."

Wiley threw him a tight smile. "She's a lovely lady."

Dax had a knowing grin on his face, but Heath and Quentin seemed to get his drift, Wiley was relieved to note.

"So, Dax, are you going to build in town, or do you want land?" Quentin asked, changing the subject.

Wiley sat back and listened with only half an ear as everyone in the group put in their two cents' worth on the advantages of living in or out of town. Instead, he thought about Jessica. It was too damn bad that the first time he'd see her would be here at the Cowboy Club. He'd have preferred a more private setting—a lot more private setting. But he couldn't very well say anything, because she'd made a big deal about them not having expectations.

Hell's bells, he had more than expectations. He had desires, strong and deep. And Lord knew, he was ready to act on them. But Jessica was wounded and she was vulnerable, and if he had to move slowly, he'd move slowly. The problem was, he had to act cool as a cucumber, pretend that there wasn't anything special going on between them, yet at the same time he wanted to make it clear to the other single guys that he'd staked her out.

He was pretty sure Quentin had gotten the message.

Heath was harder to read because he was never fazed by anything, except the occasional prospect of earning more money, which he didn't need since he never came close to spending what he had anyway. And Ford was discreet—besides, he had his hands full with his upcoming election against Myra Bridges—a fiery old battleaxe who wanted to reform everyone.

No, the biggest problem would be with Jessica herself. How the hell was he supposed to look at that beautiful face of hers and not remember kissing her? Worse, how could he keep his hands off her when the memory of their lovemaking was still so fresh in his mind?

Well, like it or not, he'd just have to find a way. He might even get a bit of help from Lady Luck. After all, he'd been the big winner at the table tonight, and Jessica would be rolling into town any time now. Who knows, before the night was over, he might be lucky in cards *and* in love.

# 6

THE BIG TRUCK rolled to a stop just past the intersection of the main drag of Red Rock. Monty glanced over at Sally Anne. "Why don't you want me to drive you to the door?" he asked.

"I think it'd be better if I walked," she replied, her heart beating nervously. "It's only a few blocks."

Monty shook his head. "Well, suit yourself." He looked in the big side mirror as a pickup went past them on the dark highway. "I think there was a convenience store in that service station half a block back. I may just walk back and get myself a cup of coffee while you're gone. Would you like something?"

She shook her head, feeling anxious. "No, thanks. I'm fine."

"Well, let me come around and open the door for you," he said.

Sally Anne waited while Jason's friend came to help her. Monty was nice, and talkative enough that she didn't have to say much. All day she'd been suffering, torn about giving up her baby, but knowing it was the right thing to do. If it wasn't for her faith in Wiley Cooper, she might have been even more uncertain, but her dad had told her that Wiley was one of the finest people ever to walk the face of the earth and she'd never seen or heard a thing to disprove it.

When the door beside her opened, Sally Anne handed down the basket to Monty. Then she climbed down. Nathaniel had been sleeping the past half hour. She was glad. Now if he'd just stay asleep until she was gone. She didn't want her last image to be of a crying baby. Nor did she want him looking at her with those big blue trusting eyes. She wanted to be able to kiss him on the cheek while he slept and wish him a happy life, confident that Wiley Cooper would make it so.

"How long will you be?" Monty asked.

"Ten minutes," she replied. "Fifteen at the most."

"All right. I'll be here."

Sally Anne nodded, then headed up the street toward the business district, walking by the light of the corner lamppost. It was late on a weeknight, so she didn't see anyone around. That was good. Not that it would be the end of the world if somebody noticed her, but the truck could be traced.

Her legs were stiff from sitting, but worse was being emotionally wrung-out. She knew that once she left Nathaniel, the pressure building inside would come pouring out. She'd probably cry all the way to Phoenix, and for a month after she got there. But this was the right thing to do, she was absolutely sure of it. That didn't make it easy, though.

WILEY GOT UP from the poker table and stretched, a broad grin on his face. "You guys sure you don't want to play a couple more hands?" he asked. "I don't want to be accused of not giving you a chance to get your revenge."

Quentin hesitated. "I'd like to, but I have to be at the Lone Eagle Ranch first thing tomorrow morning for a breakfast meeting with Julia and Erica. I'd really hate to miss a chance at Rosita's huevos rancheros. Besides, more marketing data on the ghost-town project has come in and we really need to evaluate it." Quentin and Julia Sommers were working together in developing a small theme park on the edge of Red Rock. Erica was the marketing consultant on the project.

Wiley shrugged. "Suit yourself. But early to bed and early to rise will shut down the poker game every time. That's what Grandpappy always said."

Wiley was doing his best to sound cavalier. Actually, the game couldn't end soon enough as far as he was concerned. He didn't want the whole bunch around when Jessica arrived. It would be bad enough with Ford standing there.

Fortunately, Heath followed Quentin's lead and soon the two of them were gone. Ford rubbed his stomach and groaned.

"I guess I overate again. Got myself a bellyache. Wouldn't you know it, the night I've got to stay and wait for Jessica."

"Judging by what Wanda said, she should be here any minute," Dax said. He looked back and forth between Ford and Wiley. "Either of you want some coffee?"

Ford shook his head. "Frankly, I think I need an Alka-Seltzer."

"Wiley?"

"No, thanks, Dax."

"Why don't we go out front? It's almost closing time and the staff will want to go home."

They filed out, entering the rear of the back dining room. There was no live music at the club on Thursdays, so the dance floor hadn't been in use. And for some reason, the dinner crowd had not been very heavy that evening, either.

Jake was tending bar, but the only customer in sight, Billy Wicks from the Conoco station, was just paying for his drink. He told everyone goodbye and headed out the door. Jake picked up a bar towel and began polishing a glass.

"What can I get you, boss?" Jake asked Dax.

"Not a thing. Go on home. I'll close up."

The bartender nodded, took a minute or so to finish his

cleaning up, then went out the back door. Wiley, Ford and Dax climbed up on bar stools. The lawyer groaned. It was obvious he was hurting. Wiley wondered if he dare suggest that Ford give him the keys to Cody's place and let him get Jessica settled in.

"You're looking a little pale, Mr. Mayor," Dax said to Ford. "How about some seltzer water?"

"Reckon I could handle that."

Dax went around behind the bar and got Ford a glass of water. Wiley glanced at his watch.

"How long ago was it that Wanda heard from Jessica? Surely it's been an hour."

Ford shrugged. "About that."

There was a noise outside as a big semi came down the street. It stopped just out of sight. Other than that, everything was quiet.

As Wiley looked out at the lonely night, he recalled the evening he had brought Jessica to the Cowboy Club for dinner. They'd been in a booth not ten feet from where he was sitting right now, and she'd looked so lovely with her deep blue eyes and dark hair. The slim red dress she'd worn had been sexy and sophisticated. Classy in a kind of understated way.

Her mood had been light that evening. But even so, he'd sensed the hint of vulnerability she carried with her. And since he'd seen her in Dallas, he'd been even more drawn to her sensitive side. It made him want to protect her, care for her. Which was another reason he was concerned now. She was out on the road, driving strange territory in the dark. He wouldn't feel easy until he knew she was safe. Preferably with him.

Unable to sit any longer, Wiley got off the bar stool and went to the plate-glass window at the front of the bar. He peered out into the dark street, hoping Jessica hadn't had more trouble. He didn't know about Ford, but he was starting to worry. He looked up and down the street.

There was no sign of Jessica, or anyone else, for that matter.

Then he thought he heard something. "You guys hear that?"

"What?" Dax said.

"That sound. A kind of humming."

They were all quiet for a moment but there was silence. Wiley rubbed his neck. "I must be tired. I'm hearing things."

Wiley stood at the window a minute longer, then he heard another sound, louder this time.

"There it is again," he said.

Dax joined him at the window. Ford struggled down off his bar stool and ambled over. All three men stood at the entrance of the club, close to where Wanda stationed herself to greet customers. Wiley glanced behind the podium where she kept the reservation book, but didn't see anything. Then he heard a sound coming from the vestibule. Dax opened the first set of doors. It was dark, but the street lamps cast some light through the outer swinging bar doors.

At first Wiley didn't see anything unusual. But then, when he glanced down, he spotted a fairly large basket in the corner. He stepped close to get a better look just as Dax flipped the light switch. Wiley blanched. Somebody had left a baby at the Cowboy Club!

"Jumpin' Jehoshaphat, where'd that come from?" Ford exclaimed as he leaned past Wiley to take a look.

"Not the stork, that's for sure," Wiley said, picking up the basket. Holding it, he stepped through the swinging bar doors and looked up and down the street again. It was empty. He glanced down at the baby, who was dressed in a little blue shirt with cowboy-boot designs on it—a boy. He was wide awake, waving his arms and gurgling. There was a note pinned to his shirt. There were also some jars of food and a bottle and some extra diapers at the foot of the basket.

"See anyone?" Dax asked.

"Not a soul." Wiley turned to take the baby back inside. Dax held the door open for him and Wiley set the basket on the bar and unpinned the note, which he handed to Ford. "You're the mayor, so I guess you should be the first to read this."

Ford seemed kind of shell-shocked, but he reached into his vest pocket and pulled out his reading glasses. "Where the hell is Myra Bridges when I need her?" he mumbled. "This would be more up her alley, I'm sure."

Wiley suppressed a grin. He turned his attention to the baby, reaching out to touch his waving hand. When the baby grabbed onto his finger, he started. Dax half laughed, but he didn't look any more comfortable than Wiley felt.

Ford harrumphed as he read the note. His eyebrows shot up and he gave Wiley a funny look. Then he silently passed the note to Dax. Dax whistled, also looked askance at Wiley, then handed him the note.

To Mr. Wiley Cooper,

Hi! My name is Nathaniel Gordon Springer and I'm nine months old. I'm real sorry to meet you like this, but my mother is hoping that you'll find a place in your heart for me.

My grandpa was Lucas Springer, and if he was still alive, I know he'd take care of me. But he's gone now, and my mother can't care for me any longer. She wants you to know that she tried real hard to do the right thing, like her daddy taught her, but she just couldn't make enough money to feed me and give me the life she wants me to have.

I want to grow up in Red Rock on the Double C, like she did. Since you're alone, she thought you might like me for company. I'll try hard to be a good little boy if you'll adopt me and raise me as your son. You won't regret it.

Please don't turn me away.

Love,
Nathaniel

P.S. My favorite food is applesauce.

He glanced up from the note. The baby—Nathaniel— was still gurgling as he waved his arms. Wiley took in the huge cornflower-blue eyes and blond hair. The kid looked like Lucas, all right.

Wiley took a deep breath, feeling like someone had kicked him in the stomach. He thought of Sally Anne, his foreman's little girl. She'd been sweet and loving, and he'd regarded her practically like kin. It had about killed him when he'd had to deliver the news that her father was dead—and all because of him. Even now, he couldn't forget how she'd stared at him with those huge blue eyes of hers, willing him to tell her it wasn't true, that it was some kind of a sick joke.

But it was true. Lucas was dead and no matter how much people tried to convince him otherwise, Wiley felt it was his fault. He had felt like that at the time and he still felt like that.

He made eye contact with Ford, then Dax. The mayor spoke first. "When's the last time you heard from Maggie and Sally Anne?"

"Nearly two years ago. Sally Anne wrote me, saying that they were going through a rough spell and asking for a loan. I could tell Maggie had dictated the note. I sent them a couple of grand and Maggie cashed the check, of course." He slowly exhaled. "If this is Sally Anne's kid, something pretty awful must have happened. She wasn't the type to get into trouble."

"There is no type," Dax said. "Good kids get in over their heads all the time these days."

Ford nodded. "I agree. The question is, what do we do now? Abandoning a baby is a crime. We'll have to locate Sally Anne, and she's going to have to face the consequences of this—assuming she really is this baby's mother. Even more urgent is finding someone to care for this kid. It's nearly midnight. Too late to contact anyone in Cortez with the child protective services." He scratched his ear. "I'll have to make a few calls in the morning to find out what the procedure is."

"But what about tonight?" Dax said.

Ford looked at him. "Can't you and Chloe take him in? It'd be good practice and it's only until tomorrow. Besides, the kid was left at the Cowboy Club and, well, you're the owner..."

Dax shook his head. "I don't think that means Sally Anne wants the kid to grow up in a bar, Ford, but nice try. Besides, we can't take him in because Chloe has a sore throat. We can't risk letting a baby get sick. How about the sheriff? Shouldn't he be responsible?"

"We could get a deputy over here, but he'd have the same problem," Ford said. "And with the sheriff himself still laid up with that ruptured appendix, they're already overburdened."

"You're the mayor," Dax said. "Doesn't that pretty much make you the official of last resort?"

"Me!" he exclaimed. "I'm an old bachelor. What would I do with a baby? Anyway, I've got a sour gut." Ford took a deep breath, obviously trying to come up with a better argument. "Wiley, it's clear from the note that Sally Anne intended you to raise the boy. I know there's no way that's going to happen, but in a moral sense, she's made it your problem—at least in the short term. So I hereby appoint you in charge of this baby's welfare for tonight."

Nathaniel squawked. All three men turned to look at him. The baby was gurgling and waving his arms and legs like crazy.

Ford grinned from ear to ear and slapped Wiley on the back. "I think that means the baby agrees with me. Congratulations, Wiley. Looks like you're a father again."

JESSICA PARKED the car in front of the Cowboy Club and sighed as she turned off the engine. She was pooped. And nervous. She'd been anguishing over Wiley all day long. Would things between them be the way they were in Dallas, or would everything be completely different now that she was in Red Rock?

Not that she was suspicious of Wiley's intentions, even if he turned out to be different on his home turf. Any change in attitude would be because of circumstances, not out of selfishness on his part. She knew him well enough to be confident of that much. So why was she so worried? Was she afraid that she was starting to care for him too much?

It was natural to want to protect yourself. But too much, and you insulated yourself from life. She'd learned that lesson the hard way. She was starting over now. In Dallas, she and Wiley had toasted to "new beginnings." And in the weeks since he had surprised her in Texas, Jessica had made that her mantra.

Although she was tired, something was holding her back, making her want to stay in the car. Why? She truly was ready to start a new life—maybe even with Wiley Cooper. So what was keeping her from going inside the Cowboy Club?

Nothing awful had ever happened there, so why did she feel this way? What was she afraid of?

And then it hit her. Her last two visits to the club had marked turning points in her life. Would this visit mark a turning point, as well? Not that there was a reason it should...but she could not deny that twice fate had taken a strange twist at the Cowboy Club. Maybe there was something about the place...

Jessica shivered. It wasn't from cold, because it was still quite warm out. She took a long, slow breath and told herself to get on with it. She was tired, that was all. Besides, there was no point in borrowing trouble.

## 7

JESSICA STEPPED UP on the wooden boardwalk in front of the Cowboy Club, liking that they hadn't ruined the Old West flavor of the town by putting in concrete sidewalks everywhere. She went through the swinging saloon doors knowing that her uncle would be inside. Though it was late, Dax Charboneau would probably be there, too, since he owned the place. She wondered if anyone else would be around.

As she passed through the darkened vestibule and stepped inside, she saw the main dining room was empty—not a surprise since it was midnight. As her eyes adjusted to the light, she heard voices. Turning toward the bar, she spotted Ford with Dax. Their backs were to her as they were talking to someone. Then, when they turned, she saw the one man she'd been almost afraid to hope would be there. Wiley Cooper!

Her eyes met his, a rush of pleasure and a secret awareness filling her. He was sitting on a bar stool, looking every bit as sexy and handsome as she remembered. But then she noticed that he was holding something wrapped up in a blanket. Jessica's eyes rounded. She wondered if that bundle could possibly be... Then it cried, and she knew she was right. Wiley was holding a baby!

"Jessica, thank God you're here," Ford said, walking over and taking her into his arms for a welcoming hug. "We were beginning to worry."

She stared over Ford's shoulder at Wiley, who now

had a rather sick look on his face. Ford pulled away from her, then led her over to the others.

"Hello, Jessica," Dax said. "Welcome to Red Rock."

"Thanks." She turned to Wiley, and looked down at the bundle in his arms. Pink baby flesh protruded from the blanket. She got a funny feeling in the pit of her stomach. "Is there something you didn't tell me, Wiley?"

He smiled weakly. "This is as big a surprise to me as it is to you."

"We found the little fellow outside not twenty minutes ago," Dax said. "Had a note addressed to Wiley pinned to his shirt."

"A girl who used to live in these parts seems to think Wiley needs a son," Ford added.

Jessica's eyebrows rose. "Oh, really?"

"It's not what you're thinking," Wiley hastily assured her. "Sally Anne's just a kid. Teenage daughter of my late foreman. She hasn't been around in several years. I've helped out the family financially in the past and I guess she figured I was the logical candidate to take on her kid."

"And are you?"

"No," he replied. "Absolutely not."

"What you've got here," Ford said, "is three fellows who don't know the first thing about babies. And, well, I guess we could use a little help."

Jessica saw the baby's hand slip from under the blanket and wave. Her stomach clenched. This past year she'd gone out of her way to avoid even looking at a baby, and here Wiley Cooper was, holding one. Jessica searched his eyes. She saw anguish but she wasn't sure if it was over the baby or her. She shifted her attention back to her uncle. "What about the authorities?"

Ford explained the limitations of small rural counties. "Eventually, we'll get it sorted out, but our immediate problem is what to do tonight."

Ford's tone was beseeching. That dismayed her in a way, because he knew what she'd gone through.

"We weren't quite sure how you'd feel about helping us," Wiley said tentatively.

Concluding that at least some of his concern was for her, she glanced down at the bundle in his arms, still not wanting to look at the baby's face. "Obviously, the prospect doesn't thrill me," she said.

"No, I can see that," Wiley said. "And I certainly understand why."

Jessica wasn't sure he did. But, in any case, she was beginning to feel like a heartless, selfish woman. Yet the baby's gurgling and cooing was evoking painful recollections. It was all she could do to keep from running out of the restaurant.

Then she realized this couldn't be any easier for Wiley than it was for her. He had painful associations of his own.

"So, what do you intend to do?" she asked him.

"See to it this baby's taken care of in the short run. And...well, maybe in the long run, too. I guess I feel a certain responsibility for the boy's mother. I was responsible for his granddad's death...Lucas Springer's."

"Nonsense," Dax said, interrupting. "No way was it your fault."

"I agree," Ford said.

Wiley shook his head. "Maybe not legally, but morally. Lucas worked for me and he was a good man."

"It was an accident," Ford said.

Jessica had no idea what they were talking about. "What happened?"

"Lucas had a great touch with animals," he told her. "Could read them real well. I had a wild horse I wanted to keep. Luke warned me that this one had a mean streak in him, but I was determined to turn the animal into a good stock horse. Against his better judgment, Luke got on the horse and was thrown. He broke his neck."

She heard his pain right along with the facts he relayed. This was an important issue to Wiley, she could tell—a very important issue. He had understood her vulnerabilities in Dallas. How could she turn him down now, when her help was what he needed?

Jessica drew an uneven breath. Her stomach was in a knot. Out of the corner of her eye she saw the little hand wave again. "Do we know why the girl abandoned him?" she asked.

"No," Dax said. "And until we locate Sally Anne, we won't have all the facts."

Jessica could see the short-term issues were the pressing ones. And it was pretty obvious she had a trio here who hardly knew one end of a baby from another. Given the hour, there weren't many options. She was the solution to the problem *if* she allowed herself to be.

There was a long silence, but Jessica didn't need to hear the words to know what all three men were thinking. She could see it on their faces. Every one of them wanted her to say, "Okay, give him to me." The question now was whether she could do it.

Jessica took a deep breath and looked directly at Wiley. "You want me to take him for tonight, don't you?"

"Do you think you can?" he asked, his deep voice steady and even.

She bit her lip, feeling a well of uncertainty. "I don't know."

"Why don't you try holding him for a minute?" Ford said.

She tensed.

"It's not fair of us to ask that of her," Wiley said. "I'll just take him home with me. Juana, my housekeeper, is partially disabled, but I'm sure between us, we'll find a way to keep him alive until tomorrow."

"I can see it'll be a lot harder on you than on the baby," Jessica said, gathering her courage. "There's no reason I can't take him for one night." She said the words bravely enough, but without real conviction. Stepping closer to Wiley, their eyes locking briefly, she pulled the blanket back to see the baby's face. "What's his name?"

"Nathaniel."

She took the infant from Wiley's arms. Nathaniel squirmed and she instinctively drew him close to her body. Despite his warmth, the scent of powder and sunshine and all those wonderful baby smells, her throat closed and her stomach furled.

It had been well over a year since she'd held a baby. The last time she'd touched Cassandra had been in the hospital morgue when she'd gone to identify the body. As long as she lived, Jessica would never forget that terrible afternoon. Her little girl hadn't had a mark on her; it was almost as if she'd been sleeping. But as Jessica's silent tears had fallen on her baby's face, she knew that nothing—no prayer, no bargain with God, nothing—would ever bring her precious child back to life.

Nathaniel gave a little cry, startling her. Jessica looked down at him, taking in his big blue eyes and his soft blond hair. If she had to guess, he was about the age Cassandra had been when she'd been killed. Jessica took a deep breath, hating this as much as she'd hated anything. But she was determined to get control of her emotions. The past was behind her now, and this child needed help. Her help. She looked again into Wiley's eyes, seeing compassion and feeling encouraged by it, but feeling off balance just the same.

"So, what do you think?" Ford said.

She turned to him. "I think we should worry about the baby first, not me."

Ford rubbed his stomach. His skin was pale and she saw beads of perspiration on his forehead. "If the matter's resolved, then why don't I run you over to Cody's place? I'm not feeling too hot."

"What's wrong, Uncle Ford?" she asked.

"Too much excitement and too much food," he replied. "Not to mention too many lousy poker hands."

Dax grabbed Ford's arm. "Hey, you aren't looking too good, partner."

Ford shut his eyes and nodded. "To be honest, I feel like hell."

"Maybe I ought to drive you home." He turned to Wiley and Jessica. "Can you two sort out the baby problem?"

"One way or the other," Wiley said. "Give me the keys to Cody's place, Ford."

Ford dug a key out of his pocket and put it in Wiley's hand. Jessica had been trying not to think of the infant in her arms, but the sounds and smells were almost overpowering. She glanced down at little Nathaniel, torn by a crosscurrent of emotion.

Wiley put his hand on her shoulder. It was the first time they'd touched. But the sensation wasn't what she'd expected, because she hadn't envisioned seeing him like this. That wasn't Wiley's fault. There was no one to blame.

"I'm sorry about this," he said softly, obviously understanding how hard it was for her.

"Can't be helped."

Ford had sagged back down onto a bar stool and Dax had gone to turn off the lights. Wiley picked up the basket Nathaniel had been in when they'd found him.

"Shall we go, then?"

She looked up into his blue-gray eyes, liking the way they kind of crinkled after years of outdoor living, and vowed to be strong. "Sure."

She gave her uncle a kiss on the cheek and called goodnight to Dax. Wiley took her arm. Damn, she thought, as they headed for the door, her intuition had been right when she hadn't wanted to come inside the Cowboy Club. Because, for whatever reason, fate had struck again.

JESSICA SAT in the back of her car, holding Nathaniel, and Wiley drove. They'd decided that would be safest for the baby since they didn't have an infant car seat, even though it meant Wiley would have to walk back to the Cowboy Club afterward to get his truck before he could head home.

The drive to the house that had once belonged to Cody James—Dax's partner before he passed away—wasn't a long one. Jessica sat numbly, trying to turn off all the emotion she felt. Wiley was silent, perhaps suffering as much as she. He couldn't have wanted her arrival to be like this any more than she did.

"Life is certainly full of surprises, isn't it?" she said, trying to make it easy for him.

"Tell me about it."

"I suppose it could have been worse."

"Like what, for instance?"

"Well, what if I'd gotten halfway here and changed my mind?" she said. "What if I hadn't showed up at all?"

"You're right. That would have been worse," he agreed. "Of course, then I could have flown down to Dallas and tried to persuade you to move here all over again."

"Maybe that would have been better," she said.

"This isn't the way I've been picturing it, Jessica."

She took heart in the sincerity of his tone, not that she would have believed any different. Even so, this situation wasn't the sort of thing that could be expected to nurture a new relationship. The baby squirmed. She had trouble looking at his little face, afraid of feeling anything, afraid of arousing those maternal instincts she'd fought so long to suppress.

So Jessica thought about Wiley instead, about another time when he'd driven her home, after they'd kissed under the willow tree. And she recalled the feel of his body later when they'd made love. It seemed as if that night was all she'd thought of the past six weeks. And yet, now here she was, with Wiley at last, but in circumstances that didn't exactly let either of them act on their feelings.

Soon Wiley parked in front of a tidy, little house. It was too dark to tell what color it was, but as long as it was clean on the inside, Jessica figured it would suffice until she sold her home in Dallas. That, at least, had been the plan.

Wiley came around the car and opened the door for her, reaching in to take the baby so that she could get out more easily. "Leave everything here," he said. "As soon as we get him settled, I'll come back for your luggage."

He handed the baby back to her then, though he kept a reassuring arm around her shoulder as they made their way to the front door. She was reminded of the day she and Geoff brought Cassandra home from the hospital. Jessica had been so happy, believing that with a new baby, her husband would finally settle down. Of course, it hadn't worked out that way.

Wiley opened the door, reached inside to turn on a light, then moved back so she could enter. Jessica stepped past him, feeling the heat of his body and taking in the faint, arousing tang of his cologne. She couldn't help wondering if this baby hadn't been abandoned at the Cowboy Club, would she and Wiley right now be on their way to the bedroom to make love?

"I'll get Nathaniel's basket so you can put him down," Wiley said, heading back out the door.

She turned to survey her new home. There was a brown couch and two green leather chairs in the room.

One wall had built-in cabinets and there were a bunch of books, photos in frames and a bar area. She stepped into the kitchen, directly off the living room, and turned on the light. The countertops were Formica, and there was a small table with two chairs and the usual appliances. She opened the fridge and saw milk, some lunch meat and a package of English muffins, her uncle's favorite breakfast food. She smiled, knowing she'd have to go to the store first thing.

Nathaniel reached out just then, his little fingers touching the skin of her neck. It was an innocent enough thing, but it sent another jolt through her. Remembrances.

Wiley was back. "Here's his basket," he said, stepping into the kitchen. "Where do you want me to put it?"

Jessica thought for a moment. "How about in the second bedroom. I haven't seen it yet, but it might be a good place for Nathaniel to stay while we take in the luggage. I'll keep him in my bedroom tonight, though."

"Sounds good." With that, Wiley headed for Cody's study. She followed him, realizing by his haste that he understood how hard it was for her to keep holding the baby. She appreciated his compassion.

When she got to the second bedroom, she looked around. There was an old oak rolltop desk, with a bulletin board on the wall next to it, another bookcase, and a rocking chair, in addition to the desk chair. Wiley set the basket on the floor and Jessica leaned over and carefully laid the baby in it. He immediately shut his eyes. She felt relief at being free of him.

They both tiptoed out of the room, leaving the door slightly ajar so they could hear him if he cried.

"No telling how long he'll sleep," she said. "I'm sure I'll have to get up at least once in the night to feed and change him, though."

Wiley faced her, looking sad. "I'm so sorry things have gotten off to such a bad start," he said.

"How important is that in the relative scope of things?"

"Very important," he said. Then he gathered her into his arms, holding her to his chest. He kissed the top of her head, just as he had in her kitchen back in Texas, and Jessica felt herself relax for the first time since she'd arrived. This was what she'd anticipated; this was what she'd hoped for.

"I've missed you," he said.

She looked up at him. "I've missed you, too."

Taking her chin, he kissed her lightly on the lips. As the kiss deepened, they heard a squawk from the spare bedroom. They both glanced that way. Wiley smiled, so did she. They started to resume their kiss, when the baby gave a wail. Now Wiley's expression was a bit strained.

"I'd better go have a look at him," Jessica said.

There was a flicker of disappointment on Wiley's face, but then he nodded. She went in and lifted Nathaniel from his basket. The poor little thing seemed to be wet. She put him down, then pulled one of the extra disposable diapers out of the basket. She proceeded mechanically, trying to keep her mind on the task and off all the painful associations.

Over a year ago, she'd been able to do this without thinking, and she tried hard to recapture that same frame of mind now. Once the baby was changed and dressed again, she held him, fighting those haunting feelings of love.

Glancing up, she saw Wiley, leaning against the doorframe. She brushed a loose strand of hair off her forehead. Wiley continued to stare at her.

"What?" she said.

He shook his head. "You don't want to hear."

"Yes, I do want to hear. What are you thinking?"

"No," he said, shaking his head again.

"You think I look natural doing this, don't you?"

He nodded reluctantly.

"Well, there's a reason for that, Wiley."

"I know," he said sadly.

"I really hate this," she said, her face starting to crumple.

Wiley looked as though he hated it, too. That made her feel even more sad and she began to cry. He came over to her, and put his hand on her shoulder.

"Want me to make some calls? There's got to be someone in town who'll take this kid for the night."

Shaking her head, she got control of herself and put the baby back in his basket. "No, if I can't handle this, I'll be an emotional cripple the rest of my life."

They went back into the tiny front room. Jessica plopped down in an easy chair. She was exhausted.

"I'll bring in your things," Wiley said.

It took several trips, but he got everything inside. Jessica, who hadn't moved, glanced at him mournfully. She wanted to think about Wiley—to test her feelings for him now that they were together again—but that baby in the next room kept intruding.

He stood with his hands on his hips, regarding her. She couldn't help wondering if he was having some of the same thoughts, but when he spoke, he said, "I was thinking that you'll need to go to the store in the morning to get more food for the baby."

"Yes. I was thinking that myself. He'll need more diapers," she said. "The ones in his basket won't last long."

"Yeah. Well, how about if I come by and take you?"

Her first thought was of Geoff and how they used to go to the market together. But all she said was, "Okay."

Wiley nodded. There seemed to be something else he wanted to say, but couldn't.

"How long do you think it'll take to find a place for the baby, a foster home or whatever?"

"Gee, I don't know, Jessica. This is all uncharted territory. Believe me, I'll do everything I can to see that it's done quickly. I know it's a lot more painful for you than for me, but I'm not liking this either."

"But you feel responsible because of who the girl is."

Wiley lowered his head. "Unfortunately."

"Well, what time do you want us to be ready?" she asked.

"Why not call me when you get up? I'll be here by the time you and the baby are dressed."

"Sounds good to me."

Jessica went with him to the door. Wiley pushed back a strand of her hair and kissed her forehead. Then he kissed her lightly on the lips.

"You're a real trooper," he said.

She gave him a wan smile.

He did not appear to want to go. Nor did she want him to leave. There was a moment of hesitation with emotion flowing in both directions. She swallowed hard then, looking into his eyes, almost willing him to kiss her. Wiley must have sensed how much she wanted him, because she saw the smile in his eyes as he leaned down to press his mouth to hers. At first his lips were so gentle it was as if the wind was caressing her.

She moved forward, wanting more of him. Wiley responded at once, pulling her closer until they were pressed against each other. His leg was between hers, and Jessica liked the pressure of his thigh against her mound. The kiss deepened and she thought of the night in Dallas when he'd carried her to the bedroom and made love with her.

When it was over, Wiley didn't immediately pull away. But he didn't kiss her again, either. Instead, he kissed her cheek and then whispered, "It'll all work out. I promise you."

# 8

JESSICA COULD HEAR her baby crying. She sat up suddenly and looked around. Moonlight was streaming through the window, but even though she could see clearly, nothing looked familiar. Hearing the cry again, she looked for a crib—some sign, any sign, of Cassandra. Then it hit her. Her daughter was gone. The baby was Nathaniel.

Jessica swung her legs over the side of the bed and turned on the small lamp that was on the antique oak nightstand. The baby was in his basket on the floor by her bed, his red face contorted as he chewed on his fist, wailing to high heaven. Sighing, Jessica leaned over to pick him up. His body was stiff with frustration and anger, or perhaps unhappiness. And he was hot. Jessica glanced at the clock. It was 4:00 a.m.

An hour earlier she had fed and changed him and, fortunately, he had gone right back to sleep. She'd been grateful for that, and not only because she was dead tired. Taking care of Nathaniel, touching and holding him, brought back too many memories. Memories she wasn't ready to face.

The last time she'd gotten up, as she'd grabbed a disposable diaper, she had tried to focus on work, that she'd have a lot of catching up to do with Ford's client list and caseload. She had struggled to recall how much of the practice her uncle had said was devoted to basic business law, and how much to routine torts or contract matters. For once, though, concentrating on work didn't insulate her from either her feelings or her memories. That had been a shock, because since the awful day of the accident, thinking about the law had been her salvation.

In Dallas, when she'd start to play the "should have, could have" games, she would make herself concentrate on a particularly complicated case. For the most part, that strategy had worked. And for the past few months she'd found that each week she was letting go a little more.

But maybe she'd been fooling herself about how far she'd come in her grieving. In her desire to start a new life in Red Rock, she was certain that she'd put her losses into perspective. She was ready to move on. Being with Wiley had proved that. Even though she'd been tentative at first, she had really wanted to make love with him. And in the six weeks since they'd been together in Dallas, she'd thought of him almost constantly.

Now she realized that having let go of Geoff and their marriage didn't necessarily mean that she'd finished grieving for Cassandra. In her mind, she'd made the mistake of lumping the two together. Yet, if her reaction to Nathaniel told her anything, it was that babies were still a big issue for her.

So, an hour earlier when she changed Nathaniel's diaper, instead of thinking about the law, she found herself recalling how tentative she and Geoff had been when they'd first brought Cassandra home from the hospital. They had almost been afraid to touch her for fear she'd break. Of course, within days Jessica had felt like an old hand at diaper changing, dressing, feeding and bathing her daughter. But all those tasks had seemed daunting at first.

That had made her wonder about Sally Anne. If taking care of an infant had made both her and Geoff insecure, what must it have been like for a poor teenager on her own? Terrible, she was sure. The miracle was that Sally Anne had done as well as she had for as long as she had.

Nathaniel let out a piercing wail, reminding Jessica that she'd better tend to him now. She checked his diaper but he was dry. Then she noticed again how he chewed his fist. And he was drooling like crazy. The poor thing was teething and he was obviously miserable.

Holding Nathaniel close to her breast, she knelt on the carpet and began rummaging through his basket, hoping to find an ointment to rub on his gums to ease the pain. There was nothing. Either Sally Anne hadn't been aware that there were products to help a teething baby, or she hadn't had the money to buy them.

That was so sad; the notion made Jessica want to cry. Life could be damn unfair, even to innocent babies. And to their mothers, as well. It wasn't a difficult stretch for her to imagine the depth of the pain Sally Anne must have felt upon deciding to give up her baby. Her act had either been motivated by pure desperation, or it was a manifestation of unselfish love and devotion. Maybe both.

Knowing what the poor girl must have gone through—and was probably still going through—made her shiver. She hoped that Wiley or the sheriff or the local child welfare people—whoever was going to be responsible for this—would make sure that Sally Anne didn't fall through the cracks. The girl was wrong to have abandoned her baby, but she was just a kid herself. There was no doubt in Jessica's mind that Sally Anne needed help, too.

Nathaniel took his fist out of his mouth long enough to beat it against her breast. "Oh, you agree with me, do you?" she said to him. "You don't think life has been so fair, either to you or your mommy. Well, you're right. And it's probably a mistake to let you believe it's going to be any different in the future, but there's no harm in hoping, is there?"

For an answer, Nathaniel let out another wail. Jessica

groaned as she got to her feet. "Well, let's see what we can do about that nasty old tooth, shall we?"

She recalled the way she'd often tied some cracked ice in a washcloth for Cassandra to chew on. Her mother had passed on the tip to her, and Jessica had been pleased and relieved when the approach had worked. She hoped that Nathaniel would get some comfort from it, as well.

A clean but worn linen tea towel she found in a kitchen drawer seemed both thin enough and strong enough to do the trick. She tore the towel in two, put some ice chips in the center of the cloth, then tied it so there was a bulge of crushed ice with a big enough tail attached so that Nathaniel couldn't swallow or choke on the cloth. When she handed it to him, the baby immediately stuffed the cold tea towel in his mouth. The wailing stopped and he began trying to gnaw on the ice. She silently thanked her mother.

As a teenager, Jessica hadn't fully realized the challenge her mother had faced when her father had died suddenly. Oh, she'd been aware that her mother relied on Ford for help in making decisions, but she'd never given much thought to how hard the nights must have been, lying awake alone in bed, her life turned upside down, facing the prospect of going back to work to support them.

After Geoff and Cassandra died, Jessica had told her mother that she now truly did understand what the poor woman had gone through. And, typically, Frances had nodded and said, "Yes. But it's a lesson I'd hoped you'd avoid, Jessica, especially since you've had to endure a double loss."

"Well, Mom," Jessica said, "what should I do now? What should I do with this baby?" She would call her mother soon to let her know the move had gone well. But for now she had to deal with this situation herself.

She didn't need a psychic to tell her the answer. Inside her head, Jessica heard her mother's voice, steadily urging her to do the best she could, and then to pray that it would be good enough. But what did "doing her best" mean? How far was she obligated to go for a child that wasn't hers? How much pain should she have to face in the name of compassion? It wasn't a question Jessica could easily answer.

Sighing, she cradled Nathaniel in one arm as she made up a second mini ice bag and put it in the freezer so that it would be ready when he needed another one. Then she walked into the front room of the tiny bungalow that was her new home and sat down in one of the two big green leather chairs, still holding the baby.

She hadn't turned on a light in the living room, but the lamp in her bedroom was bright enough to help her make out the major pieces of furniture. The room was tidy, a man's place to be sure. There were no flowers, no soft colors or pictures that spoke of a woman's touch. How odd, she thought, that of all the places in the world, she should end up like this—in the home of a man who'd once owned the Cowboy Club, and holding a strange baby in her arms.

That made her think of the Cowboy Club again, and Chloe Charboneau, the owner's wife. She met Chloe the night she'd gone dancing with Wiley. Chloe was a custom-shoe designer from New York. Jessica had admired a pair of silver dancing slippers Chloe was wearing and they'd starting talking. They'd hit it off, and Jessica had been looking forward to getting to know her better, figuring that as professional women, they'd have a lot in common.

Jessica rolled her neck to get out a kink, then glanced at the baby. He was wide-awake, totally preoccupied with sucking on the ice. Suddenly, as she looked down at him, she was filled with such longing, such an overwhelming desire to mother him, that it blocked out everything. Before she could even get used to the feeling, she felt a rush of hot, sharp pain. She recalled the doorbell ringing and the Texas Ranger standing there, saying there'd been an accident...and then much later, when she and her mother had gone to the funeral home to pick out the tiny, white coffin for her daughter...

No. No. No. She squeezed her eyes tight, though a tear escaped anyway. Never again did she want to risk feeling that kind of pain—the searing emptiness that didn't go away. Even if it meant she'd never again know the joy of motherhood, she simply could not face the possibility of another loss.

Looking at Nathaniel, she tried hard not to think of him as a needy little baby. He was simply a human being in trouble, and she'd do what she could for him...at least for tonight. But he wasn't her problem. He wasn't her child. She didn't love him. In fact, she didn't want him in her life at all.

WILEY LOOKED at the clock on his bedstand—5:00 a.m. He'd been awake for an hour, thinking about Jessica, worrying about Sally Anne and the baby, wondering how he'd ever juggle things to make everyone happy. Not that he considered it his duty to put a smile on folks' faces, but these particular people mattered. He cared about them.

Maybe too much.

Lord, less than twenty-four hours ago he'd gotten up feeling he was on the verge of a whole new life. Knowing that Jessica would finally be back in Red Rock had filled him with joy.

But Sally Anne's baby was throwing a wrench into the works and nothing was happening quite the way he'd planned. Not that he'd assumed that as soon as Jessica got into town they'd hop straight into bed, but he had hoped that once they were alone, things might move in that direction. When he'd kissed her last night, she'd felt that way, too. He'd have bet the ranch on it.

The baby had ruined everything.

Wiley had no sooner had that thought than he felt guilty. None of this was that poor little boy's fault. Nathaniel was innocent. So, in a way, was Sally Anne. If Lucas hadn't died, his daughter might not have gotten into trouble in the first place. And since Wiley was responsible for Lucas's death...

No matter how he looked at it, it always came back to the fact that this was on his plate. He hadn't meant it to happen, but he'd set off the chain reaction that began with Luke getting killed and ended with Jessica stuck taking care of Nathaniel. It had made him feel like the worst kind of heel to ask her to help him out, knowing that being around a baby—any baby—was painful for her.

Which was why he was determined to solve this problem...and the sooner the better.

He'd start with Juana. Later this morning, when his housekeeper came to make his breakfast, he'd ask if she knew of anybody willing to move in and care for a nine-month-old on an interim basis. Fortunately, money wouldn't be a problem. Still, money couldn't make the situation go away. Nor could it erase his memory of the haunted look he'd seen in Jessica's eyes as she'd held the baby boy in her arms.

Drawing a long breath, Wiley checked the clock on his bedstand again. Five-ten. He'd have to get up in a few minutes anyway, so he might as well get a head start on his day. Heaven knew, there was plenty to do. Throwing back the sheet, Wiley decided to take advantage of the quiet to go downstairs to his study and work on an article for the *Recorder*. On the drive back to the Double C the night before, it had occurred to him that he should put out a special edition of the paper, telling everyone about Nathaniel. The story was big news—at least in Red Rock.

He would also take the opportunity to make a few phone calls and see if his friends at the larger newspapers in Colorado would pick up the story. If so, they might hear from someone who knew where Sally Anne was, or even from Sally Anne herself. At the least, it would be one way of letting her know that Nathaniel was healthy, safe and in good hands.

Twenty minutes later, Wiley had showered and dressed and was in his study, working on the article. The banner headline, "Baby Left At Cowboy Club" was the easy part. But for once, writing the piece did not come easily to him. The reason was obvious—he was emotionally involved. Which, of course, made it all the more imperative that he handle the situation right. He was still fiddling with the opening paragraph of his story when there was a knock on his office door. It was Juana.

"Good morning, *señor*. You wish to have breakfast now, or a little while later?" she asked.

Wiley turned away from his laptop and looked directly at her so she could read his lips. Juana was partially deaf and also had a tremor that made cooking a bit of a challenge. She handled the house well, but he hadn't wanted to add the strain of caring for a baby.

"Morning, Juana. Whenever you are ready will be fine."

"Then I will heat up the griddle now for your pancakes. The coffee is almost ready. Do you want me to bring some in here?"

He nodded. "Sounds good. But before you leave, I want to ask you something. You wouldn't happen to know of anyone who'd like a temporary job taking care of a baby, would you? A little boy about nine months old."

"*Señor?*"

He told her the gist of what had happened the night before at the Cowboy Club. Juana was as upset as he had been to learn that the baby was Sally Anne's. Juana had been very fond of the girl.

"*Señor*, why did you not bring him home?"

"I didn't want to add to your burdens, Juana, not to mention my own." Wiley knew she was the type of person who would have sat up all night watching the baby, knowing she wouldn't have been able to hear him cry. And, had something gone wrong...

"This is truly terrible," she said, her hand trembling. "We must help. Everyone in town must help." She paused for a minute, her forehead creasing. "I think maybe a good person to talk to is Pastor Cole. She would know who might take care of a baby. But what of Sally Anne? How can we help her if we don't know where she is?"

Wiley heard genuine distress in Juana's voice. He could see she'd zeroed in on the heart of the problem—no surprise since Juana was a very wise and loving woman. She was in her sixties now, and had never married. She'd been with his parents from the time she was a young girl. Wiley was lucky to have her, and he knew it.

"I don't know. But I'll tell you this right now, Juana. As soon as I get the baby squared away and cared for, I'll be doing everything in my power to track down Sally Anne. You can count on it."

She nodded, satisfied with his promise. "After breakfast, maybe I should look in the storage room. We might have some of Lindsay's things. There is her crib, I'm certain. And I'll see if one of the men can get it cleaned and painted."

The mention of his daughter's crib brought a pang of regret, but Wiley pushed it back, down in that place where he put all the uncomfortable feelings he didn't want to deal with, just as he'd been doing for the past twenty years. Even as he did that, it brought to mind how much worse this had to be for Jessica than it was for him. Her loss was so much fresher.

"That's a good start," he said, looking directly at Juana. "And your idea about contacting Jamie Cole is even better. You're right. She'd know who might be able to take care of the baby. I'll call her right after breakfast."

Juana went into the kitchen then, and Wiley turned to his computer once more. But the damage had been done. He'd been worried about Jessica and Sally Anne and the baby before. Now he was thinking about another little girl, too—his daughter. Only Lindsay wasn't such a little girl anymore. She was a grown woman. Out there somewhere, living her own life, oblivious to his existence.

Would that ever change? he wondered. Or were he and Jessica doomed to go through life with a mutual heartache—the loss of their children? That gave them a bond, but it was negative. He wanted more for them than that. Which meant the real question was whether he could find a way to turn a negative into a positive. He hoped so, because this was one battle he didn't want to lose.

# 9

"THIS IS TERRIBLE, Wiley," Jamie Cole said over the phone. "The entire community needs to get involved, and I mean now, at once. Sally Anne is one of our own, and she needs to know she's not alone. In the interim, I'll do everything I can to find someone to take care of Nathaniel."

Wiley had called the tall redheaded minister of the community church right after breakfast. As expected, Jamie had been supportive. Even better, she'd understood the delicacy of the situation with regard to Jessica.

"The poor thing. What a way to start out in a new home."

"The quicker we get the baby and Sally Anne taken care of, the better it will be," Wiley said.

"I am worried about Sally Anne," Jamie said. "Goodness, she attended Sunday school at this church from the time she was a toddler. I first got to really know her when she was a preteen, just as I was finishing seminary. And I personally confirmed her a month before we buried Luke. There is no way any of us can turn our backs on her now."

"Of course not," Wiley said. "The question is, how are we going to find her? The authorities will do what they can, but this is a fairly low priority for them, and I know it. I'll contact other friends in the newspaper business and see if they'll carry the story, and maybe hire a detective, but that's about it."

Jamie paused for a long moment before she spoke. "I

might talk to some of the kids here at church she was particularly friendly with. There's a chance one of them might have heard from her."

"Good idea," Wiley said. "Maybe I'll check with Norm Jenkins over at the high school. As principal, he could maybe get me a photo from one of the old yearbooks. And he might talk to some of the teachers and find out who Sally Anne hung out with there."

"It's a start. But don't forget Maggie. She probably knows a lot more than she'll be willing to let on."

Wiley grimaced, realizing the truth in that. He recalled the note Sally Anne had sent him, asking for money. He'd have bet the ranch that Maggie had put her up to that—it sure wasn't Sally Anne's style. The real question was why Maggie hadn't written the letter herself. He'd have helped her out, given her the same amount of money. Hell, as Luke's widow, she could do no less.

Then it occurred to him that maybe Maggie had something to hide, something that reflected poorly on her, and she'd used Sally Anne as a front. Damn! Why hadn't he thought of that before? If he'd done a little investigating instead of simply salving his conscience by sending a check, maybe Sally Anne wouldn't have gotten into this fix in the first place.

Which was still another reason why he was personally responsible for this mess.

Wiley heard a click over the line, signifying that another call was coming in. "I'd better let you go now, Jamie. I've got another call and it's bound to be Jessica. I don't want her thinking I forgot about helping her out."

"Talk to you later," Jamie said.

Wiley clicked the phone and said hello. Jessica's voice was clear but ragged when she said good morning.

"Bad night?" he asked, feeling another rush of guilt.

"We're teething," she said wearily. "And I do mean 'we' since it is most definitely a joint effort. I supply the ice, Nathaniel gnaws on it with a vengeance. Until last night, I don't think that kid had ever met an ice cube, but he's a pro at chewing them now."

Wiley chuckled, liking that she was trying to put on a game face even when he knew she had to have spent a miserable night.

"Well, I can't make any promises on when, but the cavalry is definitely on the way. I talked to Jamie Cole, pastor of the community church, and she's going to see what she can do about finding a permanent nursemaid for Nathaniel."

Wiley heard a sigh of relief, and wondered if things weren't even tougher for Jessica than she'd let on.

"That's good to hear. Ford's been working on the situation, as well. He phoned me from Cortez. He sounded like he'd had a lousy night, too, what with his upset stomach and all, but he managed to make it to court anyway and he promised he'd check on procedure for dealing with this sort of situation."

"Great."

"Yes," Jessica said, "but the not-so-good news is that he had to contact local law enforcement. Apparently, Sheriff Scofield is ill, but Ford spoke with one of the deputies, Russ Something-or-other—"

"Russ Caulfield. Scofield's second in command."

"Yes. Anyway, Russ came by and talked to Ford at his office before he left for law-and-motion court. Russ wants to take statements from you and Dax, too. He's taking this very seriously. He even took Sally Anne's note with him, as evidence."

"I'd have expected that. Scofield runs a tight ship."

"Well, it may be tighter than Sally Anne would like before this is over. She's in hot water, Wiley. And there is no way you or Ford or anyone else can protect her from that. It's a crime to abandon a baby—child endangerment, possible child abuse. You get the idea."

He groaned. "I know. And I realize Ford had an obligation to contact the authorities."

"Good. I was sure you'd understand." She paused for a moment. "At least we'll have a better idea of what's to become of Nathaniel when Ford returns from Cortez. He promised to get back to me sometime after lunch today with a report on what he learned over there."

"That is the first step, I suppose." He rubbed his chin, thinking. "Not to change the subject, but I assume you still need supplies. If you're game, how about if I head for town and drive the two of you to the market? Then, if you don't mind, we can drop by the paper. I need to take some photos of the baby for the front page of a special edition I want to put out. We can grab a bite of lunch afterward."

She didn't say anything.

"Jessica?"

"Oh, yeah. Fine, Wiley."

"Is there a problem? I don't want you taking on anything you're not comfortable doing."

"No, I'll do what's necessary to help this baby. And it *will* be nice having adult companionship and a little intelligent conversation after a night of cooing and baby talk. Lunch sounds great. Whenever you get here, we'll be ready, ice and all."

Wiley chuckled at her last words and hung up. In spite of his laughter, he couldn't help thinking that between Jessica's stabs at humor, and her attempt to try to put the best light on the situation, there was something else in her voice. It wasn't just stress. It was more like raw pain.

The way Wiley figured it, he owed Jessica. The best way to show her how much he appreciated her sacrifice was to make sure that her burden would be lifted as soon as possible. But would that be enough? he wondered. He wasn't sure. At some level she had to resent the fact that none of this would have happened if it hadn't been for him. The possibility that would affect her feelings for him long term was not a pleasant prospect, and it ate at him.

Which made it all the more important that he solve the problem of who would take care of the baby, pronto.

Wiley's Grandpappy Cyrus would have said he was trying to ride a new path at full trot...and Cyrus would have been right. But what choice did he have?

IN ALL HER YEARS of grocery shopping, never once had Jessica encountered anything like her trip to the Four Corners Market. Within five minutes of running into the likes of one overweight woman with iron-gray hair on the far side of sixty by the name of Myra Bridges, Jessica started to wonder if pulling up stakes and moving to Red Rock would turn out to be the decision from hell.

Not that the woman wasn't friendly—in a rather officious way. But no sooner were the words, "Welcome to Red Rock," out of her mouth than the candidate for mayor wanted to know the details about everything that had ever happened to Jessica—from when and how she met Wiley, to whose baby it was in the shopping cart, why Jessica had ended up with it, and a coldly polite inquiry as to whether or not the proper authorities had been notified or was this one more instance where Mayor Lewis was letting an important problem slip through the cracks?

Jessica was worn out just listening to the woman. But at the same time, she had to hand it to her. A lot of prosecuting attorneys she knew didn't have Myra Bridges's go-for-the-jugular instincts.

Still, the cutting remark about her uncle didn't sit particularly well with her, and Jessica was about to politely but firmly put the woman in her place when Wiley stepped in, probably avoiding a minor incident. Jessica took the opportunity to make her escape, wheeling the grocery cart down the aisle at breakneck speed. Nathaniel cried out with the joy of pure excitement as she swung around a corner and went over a couple of rows to the section where baby products were sold. Unless Myra had grandchildren here in town, Jessica figured it was one place the woman wouldn't likely go.

As she slowed the cart and began heading down the aisle at a leisurely pace, she grabbed strained fruits and vegetables with one hand, while trying to keep Nathaniel's chubby little arms and legs in the cart with the other. Just as she was putting some of his favorite applesauce in the cart, she heard someone call out her name.

"Jessica? Jessica Kilmer? Is that you?"

Wondering what now, Jessica turned to see a petite, all-American-looking blonde with a ponytail. The woman was obviously pregnant, probably about five months along. Her pretty face was familiar, and certainly seemed a lot friendlier than Myra's, but Jessica couldn't place it.

"Kate MacInnes," the thirty-something blonde said, holding out her hand. "We met at the Cowboy Club when you came to town a few months ago."

"Oh, yes," Jessica said, taking a fresh box of baby wipes out of Nathaniel's mouth and putting them in the back of the cart, out of his reach. He immediately stuck his fist in his mouth and began chewing away. "You and I both fell in love with those sensational silver shoes Chloe James was wearing. As I recall, you were trying to talk your husband into buying you a pair."

"Right. And I got them, too." She patted her tummy. "The least he could do considering what he'd done to my figure. How about you? Did you order a pair?"

"Oh, yes. Though I haven't worn them yet."

"Well, that can be corrected. There are plenty of guys around town who'd love to take you dancing at the Cowboy Club tonight, I'm sure." Kate gave a meaningful look at Nathaniel. "Unless this little cowboy here means you're already taken, that is."

Kate hadn't exactly asked if the baby was hers, but the comment was close enough that Jessica flinched anyway. Pain. It always came first. Then the emptiness. That was the worst part—the unrelenting emptiness. She forced a smile, telling herself that Kate had no idea what she'd just done. No one ever did. Of course, that didn't make it hurt any less.

"He isn't mine," Jessica said, taking care to keep her voice low and even. "I just got drafted to do the baby-sitting." She gave Kate the abridged account of how she had wound up taking care of Nathaniel.

"You really *were* drafted." Kate's bright blue eyes crackled with fire. "Isn't that just like men...to assume you should be in charge of a baby because you wear the skirt? Honestly, if my husband wasn't so darned cute, I swear I'd give him the heave-ho along with the rest of the male population."

"That would be a little drastic," Jessica said, smiling.

Kate nodded. "I know. So I'm doing the next best thing. Training my boys from the get-go that women are their equals." She leaned closer to whisper confidentially, "I would really love to teach them that we're superior, but I don't think John is ready for the unvarnished truth."

Jessica giggled, liking Kate MacInnes. The thought that they might become friends gave Jessica a lift. Lord knew, she couldn't picture herself becoming bosom buddies with the likes of Myra Bridges.

No sooner had that thought crossed her mind than she heard the woman's strident, disembodied voice rise over the soft country-and-western music that was playing over the P.A. system. "Mark my words, Wiley Cooper, there'll be hell to pay around here if this isn't handled properly. And I do mean *properly*." The sound was coming from a different aisle.

Jessica heard Wiley say something placating. She couldn't make out the words, but the tone was clear. When she turned back to Kate, the woman was fanning herself and rolling her eyes heavenward.

"Lordy, that Myra Bridges will be the death of someone yet. She harangues pretty near everyone in town about something or other."

Jessica chuckled. "Well, she did a number on me earlier. Grilled me like a D.A. determined to run for attorney general."

"She's been in high gear ever since she decided to run for mayor. If you want my opinion, that makes your uncle a shoe-in. No one wants to tangle with Myra. Things are never quite right with her and she has every intention of 'rooting out evil and making Red Rock a safe place to live.'"

Jessica blinked. "Isn't it safe now?"

"You bet. Safe as houses." Kate reached over with a hankie and wiped drool off Nathaniel's chin, looking as if she had done the same thing a thousand times before with her own brood, which she undoubtedly had. "But Myra's never satisfied. To tell you the truth, the old battleax tires me out, just talking about all the 'problems' around here."

"Did I hear someone mention problems?" Wiley said, coming up behind her.

Jessica turned to him. Twenty minutes earlier, when Wiley had shown up at her door, he'd struck her as decidedly male, vital, alive. The tang of his cologne had told her he'd just shaved and showered. And his eyes had been lively. Now, after sparring with Myra, he seemed almost tired. Nonetheless, Wiley had a slow, easy way about him that had a strong effect on her. Just the sight of him sent a ripple of pleasure through her.

"Hi, Wiley," Kate said. "We were talking about Myra just now, in case you haven't figured it out."

"Kate." He glanced down at Nathaniel, then at Jessica, that look of wariness in his eyes.

"I see you're back in the baby business again," the woman said. "Wasn't ranching and running the *Recorder* enough to keep you busy?"

Wiley rubbed his jaw. "This isn't exactly my first choice for unexpected developments," he replied. "John should've been the one this little cowboy's mother picked. He's sure got the formula down. A one-man population explosion."

"Ha!" Kate said. "John's talents are mostly in the preconception phase. A baby has to walk and talk before my dear husband's useful again."

"I guess what you're telling me, Kate, is you won't be volunteering to look after Nathaniel, here." He gave Jessica a wink.

"This is my third in five years," Kate said, putting her hands on her pregnant stomach. "I'm trying to rest up. Thanks, but I'm afraid young Nathaniel is yours, Wiley."

"Only temporarily," he said hastily. He glanced at Jessica, shifting uncomfortably. "So, did John drive you into town, by any chance?" Wiley asked Kate. "I've been meaning to chat with him about an article on water rights I'm doing for the paper next month, and I'd just as soon do it face-to-face."

"Yep. He's at the barbershop with our two little barbarians while I do the marketing. But if you want to talk to him, why don't we all get together one night at the Cowboy Club for dinner and dancing instead? That would be a lot more fun. Of course, I'm not as light on my feet as Ginger Rogers nowadays, but I've got another month before I have to hang it up for the duration. Besides, Jessica and I both have new silver dancing shoes that need to be broken in."

Wiley turned to her. "I'm game. What do you think, Jessica?"

She glanced down meaningfully at Nathaniel. "Assuming that the cavalry has arrived, yes."

"Good," Kate said. "Let's plan on it. The sooner the better." She threw Jessica a sly smile, having obviously taken in the interplay between her and Wiley over the baby. But, wisely, she didn't say anything. "Well, I should get going. My boys ought to be as handsome as they're going to get by now. Give me a call and we'll set up an evening to go dancing. Nice seeing you again, Jessica."

Nathaniel began waving his arms and squawking then. His little fist was red from where he'd been chewing on it. She needed to do something about that. "Can you watch him for a minute, Wiley?" she said. "I have to find some ointment for his sore gums and also pick up a few things for myself."

"No problem," he said.

Jessica took off down the aisle. She found the gum ointment without any trouble, planning next to gather a supply of her favorite cereal, some soft drinks, and fresh fruit and vegetables. She collected a three- or four-day supply of baby food on the theory that even if she was rescued sooner rather than later, the food could always be sent along with the baby.

As she took the baby food off the shelf, she realized some dangerous feelings were beginning to creep into her consciousness. She was beginning to feel a responsibility for this baby, almost a possessiveness. It was not a place she wanted to go, especially as it was clear from the way Wiley had reacted to Kate's teasing that he was managing to keep an emotional distance.

She was about to turn away when she spotted a chain of brightly colored toy keys on a display. It reminded her of the ones Cassandra had had, and the day they'd gotten them. She and Geoff had taken Cassandra on a shopping expedition. They'd been in Wal-Mart, and Jessica had left the two of them for a minute because she wanted to see about getting a new iron. When she got back, Geoff was holding Cassandra, and she was playing with a set of bright plastic keys. Apparently she'd spied them on a display and wanted them, and Geoff had decided to buy them for her.

It had been a nice day. At the time, it had seemed rather ordinary, as so many of their days were. But ever since the accident, it had seemed to Jessica as if those ordinary days were so significant. Not Cassie's first Christmas, when she had only been home from the hospital a few weeks, or her first Easter, which had been just weeks before she was killed, but rather the quiet times when they'd gone on errands and taken walks.

Though her arms were already full, Jessica took the plastic keys off the display and made her way back to where she'd left Wiley and the baby. He was looking down at Nathaniel with consternation, clearly ill at ease, even in the baby-sitting role. Seeing her, he brightened.

"Ah, here you are," he said, taking some of the things from Jessica's arms and helping her get everything into the grocery cart.

She kept hold of the plastic keys. Seeing the brightly colored object in her hand, Nathaniel reached for it. When he let out a squawk, Jessica removed the toy from the packaging and handed it to him. The baby immediately thrust one of the keys into his mouth. Jessica and Wiley exchanged a look.

"So, are we all set?" he asked.

"Guess so."

Jessica looked at the baby, again experiencing that terrible tug in two different directions.

"You all right?" Wiley asked.

"I'm fine."

"Are you sure?"

"Well, if I seem strange, it's because I keep thinking about my daughter."

Wiley shook his head. "I'm sorry, Jessica."

"It's not your fault," she replied, gathering herself. "I have moments like this. They pass."

She indicated she was ready to go by her body language. Wiley followed her along the aisle, pushing the cart. Jessica glanced back at him, doing her best to signal that she was okay. But deep inside, she wasn't sure if she was or not. What was this baby doing to her? And could she do anything to stop it?

# 10

WILEY COULD SEE she was uncomfortable, so he took the pictures as fast as he could. Nathaniel was not in a very cooperative mood and Jessica kept handing him the plastic keys, which he chewed furiously. "Just like Cassandra," Wiley heard her murmur as she wiped the drool from the corner of the baby's mouth.

Wiley took one last shot from across the street, so that he could get in the whole Cowboy Club, then he returned to where Jessica stood holding Nathaniel. "There, that ought to do it," he said.

Jessica looked relieved.

"Look," he said, brushing her cheek with his fingers, "why don't we swing by Jamie Cole's place and leave Nathaniel there? She's working on lining up somebody to take care of him and there's no reason she can't look after him in the meantime. I don't think she'd mind, truly. You've already gone way beyond the call of duty. Enough is enough."

"We can't just pass him around like a football."

"But I can see how hard this is on you."

She smiled, clearly grateful for his concern. "I'll survive. Though if you don't mind, maybe we should skip lunch. I ought to get Nathaniel back so I can put him down for a nap."

Wiley said sure, although he felt a little frustration. He slipped his arm around her shoulders as they headed for his truck. "I can see my mistake with Lucas has spread misery a lot farther afield than I imagined."

"Well, don't blame yourself. It's just something that happened. The community is pulling together to take care of the situation. That right there says a lot about Red Rock."

"But you're the one who's stuck."

"I'd like to think I'm part of the community, too."

He gave her shoulders a squeeze. "And I, for one, am damn glad you are."

Wiley felt a little better as they made their way to Cody's house. Glancing over, he saw Jessica looking down at Nathaniel, with maybe even a hint of a smile. That made him think that all her memories couldn't be sad. Even so, she—they—needed to get on with their lives. Together. The way it had been in Dallas.

Everything there had seemed so romantic, almost larger than life. And though Jessica had been tentative and vulnerable, she'd opened to him like a flower in need of rain when he'd made love to her. It had been a wonderful night. And the next morning had been terrific, too. He recalled how he'd awakened her, kissing the back of her neck until she'd turned into his arms, ready to be taken. Lordy, he wouldn't forget that if he lived another thousand years.

Wiley sighed. Last night could have been like that. It *should* have been like that. He'd seen the light in Jessica's eyes when she'd first spotted him at the club. And he'd felt the fire in her when he'd kissed her good-night. But she was so preoccupied with this baby—and all the dark memories he had hoped to banish from her mind—that his chance of getting her mind on romance was nil. Worse, he wasn't sure what he could do to change the situation.

When they reached Jessica's rental house, Wiley carried in the groceries and Jessica held the baby. Then she gave him Nathaniel to hold while she put things away.

"I think I'll give him a bottle, then put him down for a nap," she said once the kitchen was in order.

Wiley had been seeing her domestic side, an aspect he rarely saw in a woman, excepting Juana, of course. But her comment now made him recall that she'd fixed him breakfast in Dallas. They'd eaten late, almost lunchtime, because he'd spent a good long time with her in bed that morning before they made it to the kitchen. At the time, he'd been way too preoccupied with the newness of the situation, and how it felt to be with her, to pay much attention to how she looked in a kitchen. Seeing her now, moving from the sink to the refrigerator to the cupboards, gave him another odd, possessive feeling.

When Jessica had Nathaniel's bottle ready, she took him from Wiley and they sat down at the table. The baby began sucking on the bottle eagerly. The tension eased and all three of them seemed to relax. For a while, Wiley watched in silence.

Then he said, "For a professional woman, you seem to know your way around a house."

"It's in the genes, Wiley, whether we like it or not."

"You know, I've been thinking about what Kate MacInnes said about getting together with her and John for some dinner and dancing at the Cowboy Club. Since we aren't going to have lunch together, what would you think about going tonight?"

"Tonight?"

"Yeah, why not?"

"Aren't you forgetting someone?" She glanced down at Nathaniel.

"Oh. Well, surely there's something we can do with him for a few hours. Heck, maybe by this evening Jamie will turn up somebody to take him on for the duration."

She blinked. "The duration? You mean like the next eighteen years?"

"No," he said with a laugh. "I meant until we locate Sally Anne and get everything sorted out."

The phone rang in the other room. Wiley volunteered to get it. It was Kate MacInnes.

"Hey, we were just talking about you," he said. "Thinking about going dancing. You and John have plans for tonight?"

"Actually, we're playing bridge."

"Oh. Well, it is short notice."

"How about next weekend?" Kate said.

"Yeah, that would be good. I'll ask Jessica."

"We don't have to decide now. But there is something I'd like to talk to her about."

"Sure, I'll put her on."

Wiley went to get Jessica. She handed him Nathaniel and he sat with the boy at the table. The baby had finished his bottle and looked content in his arms. Wiley stared into his innocent little face. "Well, partner, what do you think of Jessica?" he mumbled. "Seems like you're just about as fond of her as I am."

Nathaniel cooed. Wiley smiled.

"Don't get to attached to her, though. I found her first."

The baby smiled, waving his hand. Wiley had to admit he was cute—a real little cowboy. But Nathaniel Springer also posed a hell of a problem. Innocent though he was, he was complicating a whole lot of lives. Shaking his head, Wiley thought of those days long ago when his own daughter was born. Talk about complicating lives. In an odd way it was something he still hadn't gotten over. Lindsay had never truly been part of his life, but she was an unclosed chapter, an unresolved issue.

Wiley could hear Jessica ending her conversation in the next room. A moment later, she returned to the kitchen.

"That was really sweet," she said. "Kate offered me a bunch of used baby things to help tide us over."

"Why'd she do that? She's about to have her third."

"She's giving me her boy things. The baby she's expecting is a girl."

"Oh."

Jessica did not rush to take the baby back. Wiley started feeling uncomfortable.

"What's Kate offering the stuff to you for?" he asked. "We're about to get rid...I mean...Nathaniel will be going to a foster home the minute it's lined up."

"The things aren't for me. She wanted to give them to me for Nathaniel. They'll go to whomever gets him."

"Oh, I see. Makes sense. Thoughtful of Kate."

"She's very considerate," Jessica said.

Wiley noticed a smell. He saw Jessica observing as he reacted.

"The baby needs to be changed?"

"He needs something."

"Let me take care of it, then I'll put him down for his nap."

Jessica took him and went off. She seemed so capable and in charge. Wiley could tell she was starting to adjust to having a baby to care for again. Not that she seemed real comfortable with the notion, but she was now into the coping stage. He admired her for that. Fate had been good to him, despite this little cowboy coming into their lives. In fact, he had a hell of a lot to be thankful for.

JESSICA HAD PUT Nathaniel into his basket and could see that the little tyke was going to be asleep in moments. She was glad because she needed a respite. Turning for the door, she found Wiley there, watching her. He was smiling.

"You're an amazing woman," he said softly as she approached him.

"Amazing?"

"Well, let's just say I have a tremendous amount of respect for you," he said, gathering her into his arms.

Jessica gave him a hug as he kissed her temple. They held each other, looking down at the baby. Funny, but she almost felt as if Nathaniel were theirs. After all, they'd gone to the market with him, fed him, changed him. Wiley hadn't sat up in the night with her, but he'd been in her thoughts.

"Come on," he said. "We need a little time for us."

They went into the front room and sat on the sofa. Wiley put his arm around her and she leaned against him, sighing.

"I definitely think we should go dancing tonight," he said. "Kicking up your heels a little is just what you need."

"Think so, huh?"

"Damn tootin'."

She thought fondly about the wonderful night they'd spent together in Dallas. Wiley was probably remembering, too—and thinking how unfortunate it was this baby had gotten in the way. Yet, traumatic as taking care of him had been at times, Jessica was beginning to see that the experience was forcing her to address issues she'd avoided until now—things she'd kept locked tight inside, things she'd been fighting. They were still there, of course, but she was facing her pain now.

Wiley had made a difference, as well. Before he'd come into her life, she'd felt alone and empty. He had brought a sense of hope. Everything seemed to matter more. She cared. That was a wonderful gift.

Wiley skimmed the back of his fingers down the side of her neck. The sensation sent a tremor through her and she glanced up at him. He kissed her then. A hungry kiss. His hands held her firmly against him and they were both breathing heavily. The fire he'd helped her rediscover in Dallas threatened to surge out of control. She was starting to think of the bed in the next room, and Wiley must have been, as well, because he got up, pulling her to her feet.

But fate had other ideas. The phone rang.

"Oh, hell," he said. "Let it ring."

Jessica stopped. "No, it'll wake Nathaniel." She snatched up the receiver. "Hello?"

"Jessica, it's Ford."

"Hi, Uncle Ford."

She glanced at Wiley, who had a look of chagrin on his face. She playfully gave his stomach a pinch.

"Well, I've got good news," her uncle said. "Had a call from the county people in Cortez. They've found a foster home for the baby."

The news was a jolt. Surprisingly, not an altogether pleasant one. A little wave of panic went through her. "Really?"

"Yeah, there's a ranching family near Cortez that's taken in foster children before. Adopted a couple of them, even. Wilkins is their name. Don't know a thing about them, but the county people say they're good folks."

The panic was replaced by a heavy feeling in the pit of her stomach. "You say they're near Cortez? How far away is that, Uncle Ford?"

"Oh, I reckon their ranch must be fifty miles from Red Rock."

"Isn't that kind of far?"

"Far? Far for what?"

Jessica hesitated. "Well, the people of Red Rock kind of look upon Nathaniel as their responsibility. His mother came from here, and folks have sort of taken him into their hearts."

"Jessica, what in tarnation are you talking about? This family is licensed and approved to care for wards of the state. You were pressed into service on an emergency basis. I thought you'd be thrilled."

"Well, I'm glad, of course. I just think it would be better to find someone here in Red Rock to take the baby."

"What's going on?" Wiley said.

"Just a minute, Uncle Ford," she said, putting her hand over the mouthpiece. She told Ford's news to Wiley.

He seemed pleased as punch, which annoyed her. Wiley noticed.

"Isn't this what we want, a responsible family to look after him?" he asked.

"Yes, but I don't think Nathaniel should be fifty miles away."

"Why? He doesn't know the difference."

"Maybe not, but I do!"

Wiley blinked.

"What I mean is, he's Red Rock's responsibility," she explained. "Ours collectively. Look at all the people who've gotten into this."

"Jessica, not that many people even know about Nathaniel."

"Well, they will soon enough. You're putting out a special edition of the paper. Anyway, I thought you were the one with the guilty feelings. I thought you said you felt responsible."

"I said I feel an obligation to see that Sally Anne and her baby are taken care of. Getting Nathaniel into a home where he can be cared for is the first step."

"Are you saying I can't care for him properly?"

He shook his head. "Sweetheart, I'm not saying that at all. I don't think you understand. We're talking temporary solution."

Jessica stopped and took a deep breath. Wiley was right, her emotions were in a jumble. She also knew it was wrong to pack up this baby and ship him off again. She got back on the phone with Ford.

"Surely somebody in Red Rock will take him until Sally Anne is found or things are otherwise resolved," she said.

"Honey, we're lucky to find anybody at all to take him," Ford told her.

"Well, what about the minister? I thought she was going to get someone."

"Jamie Cole?"

"Yes, Wiley said she'd ask around."

"Well, speak of the devil," Wiley said. He'd gone over to the window. "Here comes Jamie now."

"Uncle Ford, I'll call you back in a few minutes. Pastor Cole just arrived."

Wiley opened the door. Jamie, looking more like a cowgirl from one of the local ranches than an ordained minister, came in, beaming. She was in jeans and boots and a western shirt, her gorgeous red hair pulled back in a thick French braid that went nearly to the middle of her back.

"You must be Jessica," she said, walking up to her. "Jamie Cole." She extended her hand. "Welcome to Red Rock."

"Thanks."

Jamie looked back and forth between them. "Got your baby problem solved, folks," she announced cheerfully. "Ruthie Thompson said she'd look after Nathaniel."

"Ruthie?" Wiley said. "She's got to be well into her sixties."

"So? You think a woman forgets everything she ever knew about kids just because she's past menopause?" Jamie said. "Ruthie had five of her own and she's got seventeen grandchildren. Since losing Mitch, she's been at loose ends. This will be good for her."

Jessica felt a surge of relief. She had no idea who

Ruthie Thompson was, but she was local, and that was good enough, especially if the minister herself recommended the woman. Jessica beamed at Wiley, who looked as though he didn't know what to think.

"I wonder if the county will go along with this," he said.

"Let me talk to Ford," Jessica said, returning to the phone. As she dialed, Wiley explained to Jamie what was going on.

"Law offices," Ford said, answering his phone himself. Jessica wasn't surprised, because Judy, his secretary, only worked part-time.

Jessica gave him Jamie's news.

"I don't know how they're going to feel about that in Cortez," Ford said. "It's not exactly the federal government over there, but they do have their rules and procedures."

"Surely you can convince them, Uncle Ford. You know Ruthie Thompson, don't you?"

"Certainly. I've done all of hers and Mitch's legal work for years. I'm handling the probate of his will."

"She's responsible and competent, isn't she?"

"Yes, but that's not the issue."

"Uncle Ford, are you telling me they won't listen to you over in Cortez?"

"I'm not telling you any such thing, young lady. I can probably get them to agree, for a few days anyway. What I don't understand is why you've got a bee in your bonnet over this."

"Let's just say that I feel like a responsible citizen of Red Rock."

"I'll call you back in a few minutes if I can get through to the right people."

"Okay."

Jessica hung up, explaining to Wiley and Jamie what was going on. Jamie said she had a house call to make on a shut-in and couldn't wait for word from Ford. "Depending on the outcome, you can call Ruthie directly and let her know," she told Wiley.

"I'll take care of it," he said.

Jamie said goodbye and gave Jessica a hug before going.

"What a nice lady," Jessica said, sitting on the sofa.

Wiley dropped down next to her. He gave her a penetrating look. "What was that about, Ms. Kilmer?"

His question surprised her. "What do you mean?"

"Ford had everything worked out and you threw a monkey wrench into the works."

She frowned. "I did not. I'm simply trying to do what's best for an innocent child that's been left in my care—at *your* request, need I remind you, Mr. Cooper."

"That's not what I mean."

"Oh. Then, what do you mean?"

Wiley looked as if he was having trouble finding a way to say it. Finally he spoke. "You've gotten attached to that kid, haven't you, Jessica?"

"*Attached?*"

"Yes. Attached. Why else would you balk at the solution Ford worked out?"

"I told you. Because—"

"No," he said, cutting her off. "Fifty miles is important to you, not Nathaniel."

She glared at him, ready to deny the charge. Then she realized maybe he was right. But so what? If you cared about a human being's welfare, then you did. "Maybe I would like to know he's nearby."

"Why?"

"So I'd feel better. I don't see what's so strange about that," she said. "In fact, I'm surprised you wouldn't prefer it yourself, considering your relationship with Sally Anne."

Wiley contemplated her. She knew he was exposing

some contradictions in her feelings, but they were honest contradictions. No law said a woman couldn't feel torn about something, especially when that something was a baby.

"Maybe my reaction seems strange to you," she admitted, "but I'm wondering why you're making such a big deal out of it. Is there anything you're afraid of?"

"Afraid?"

"Yes. I almost get the feeling you feel threatened by my concern for Nathaniel."

"Not at all," he said almost too quickly.

"Really?"

"Yes, really."

Now she was the one who studied him.

"What?"

"Wiley, let me ask you something. What if, when you came over this morning, I told you that Nathaniel was the cutest thing in the world, and that I wanted to keep him?"

His eyebrows rose. "Is that how you feel?"

There was a hint of terror in his voice. She heard it. "No, it's not. I've told you exactly how I feel. I just wanted to know what you'd think."

"I thought we were pretty much in the same boat, Jessica. We've both had losses in connection with our children. I...well, let's say I feel an obligation to look out for Luke's child and grandchild, but it stops with seeing that they're provided for."

"That's how I understood you to feel," she said calmly.

"So, do we have a problem or don't we?"

She shook her head. The phone rang.

"You get it," Jessica said, feeling an odd tug of emotion she didn't fully understand.

"Hello?" Wiley said. He listened for a minute. "Okay, Ford, I'll tell her." Wiley put down the phone and returned to the sofa. "The county people were a little reluctant but they agreed to let us keep the baby in Red Rock for a few days. Somebody will come by tomorrow to talk to Ruthie and have a look at the baby."

Jessica was pleased, though she couldn't exactly say why.

"Shall I call Ruthie and let her know?" Wiley asked.

"Yes, please do."

"And when do you want to take the baby to her?"

The question seemed almost cruel, though she knew Wiley didn't mean it that way. It didn't matter to him whether Nathaniel was in Cortez or Red Rock as long as he was well cared for. But her motives were different. She had feelings that ran deeper. What they were, exactly, were a mystery…even to her.

"Jessica?"

"Oh. Well, how about after he wakes up from his nap?"

Wiley nodded, getting up and returning to the phone. He didn't know Ruthie's number so he had to call information. Jessica listened to him talking, realizing that she had to undo the emotional ties she had already formed with the baby, or risk being hurt again. That wouldn't be easy, because she'd rediscovered her instinct to love.

## 11

RUTHIE THOMPSON proved to be a typical grandmother, rosy-cheeked and cheerful. She was wearing an apron and a bright blue housedress when she answered her door. Jessica held Nathaniel in her arms as Wiley stood behind her, having lugged all the baby supplies and the basket from his truck.

"There's the little cowboy," Ruthie said, peeking in the blanket, her blue eyes twinkling then going back to Jessica. "You must be Ford's niece."

"Yes, I'm Jessica Kilmer."

"Come in, dear, come in."

Ruthie held the door open for Wiley and greeted him, as well.

Baking smells permeated the tiny little cottage. It reminded Jessica of her mother's place. She looked down at Nathaniel who was awake and wide-eyed, but silent. His innocent little face sent a twinge of anxiety through her. Jessica admonished herself. This was what she'd told herself she wanted—to be free of all the painful reminders of Cassandra. Yet, for some reason, she was finding it difficult to put Nathaniel in a stranger's arms.

Ruthie moved closer for a better look at the boy. "What a fine-looking young man," she said. "And so well behaved."

"He can get cranky," Jessica warned. "Be prepared to lose some sleep."

"All babies seem to have one thing or another. Is he teething?"

"To put it mildly."

Ruthie was obviously ready to hold him, so Jessica eased him into her arms. She cuddled and cooed at him, poking his fat little cheek with her finger. Nathaniel actually smiled, which made Jessica grin with pride before she caught herself, realizing there was no reason for her to be feeling anything but relief.

While Ruthie continued to rock the baby in her arms, Jessica went over his eating habits, sensitivities, the supplies and the medications she'd brought. "I guess the county people are coming to see Nathaniel tomorrow, but it seems to me it'd be a good idea if a pediatrician had a look at him, as well. I'd be happy to take care of the expense."

"That's real generous of you, sweetheart, but I thought the whole purpose of me taking the little tyke was to get the burden off your shoulders."

Jessica drew a long breath, glancing at Wiley, who'd been silently observing. "Well...yes, that's true," she said, "but...I feel a certain responsibility. Maybe we owe it to each other to share the burden."

"Whatever you want to do is fine," Ruthie said.

"Is there anything else we need to discuss?" Wiley asked.

Jessica could see he was gearing up for them to leave. "No. Unless Mrs. Thompson has any questions, I'm ready to go."

Ruthie beamed. "I'm sure Nathaniel and I will get along just fine. You two headed out for dinner?"

"Cowboy Club," Wiley said.

"Oh, what fun!"

Jessica and Ruthie exchanged smiles. Jessica shot Nathaniel a final furtive glance, reached over on an impulse and gave his hand a squeeze. "Thanks so much, Mrs. Thompson," she murmured, then headed for the door before she began to cry.

Wiley caught up with her on the walk, and put an arm around her waist. "You okay?"

"I'm fine," she said, brushing away a tear.

He opened the door of the pickup and helped her into the cab. Then he went to the driver's side and climbed in. He regarded her. "It's my fault you had to go through that, Jessica. I'm sorry. I'll do my best to make it up to you."

"Don't be silly. I've been overly emotional over this. That's all."

Wiley extended his hand, and she took it. He was being very sweet. She managed to smile.

"So, how does a nice meal and some dancing sound?"

"Wonderful," she said, brightening.

Wiley nodded, indicating he shared her enthusiasm. He started the engine, looking in the side mirror before pulling into the street. Jessica glanced up at Mrs. Thompson's house, telling herself this was the way it was meant to be. If she was smart, she'd never see little Nathaniel Springer again.

THE EVENING WAS TURNING out to be everything Wiley had hoped it would be. There'd never been a time when he'd taken a woman to the Cowboy Club and they hadn't both had a good time. But with Jessica, the place seemed extra special. Maybe more romantic. He looked around, wondering why that was. The long mahogany bar with the gilt mirror over it looked the same as always. The deer and buffalo heads on the walls gave the place real Wild West color, but he was used to that since he'd been coming here his whole life.

Wanda had seated them in a booth close to the dance floor, just as he'd asked. They'd had a terrific dinner. Jessica had finally gotten the steak she'd wanted ever since that solitary meal she'd eaten in Dallas right before he'd shown up at her place. Wiley had ordered the buffalo stew, which had a rich red wine sauce and rock shrimp in it—his favorite dish.

They'd danced three songs in a row and he was getting more curious stares than he could ever recall. Of course, he knew that folks were speculating about the beautiful raven-haired woman with the startling blue eyes. He was content to leave them guessing—Lord knew, he didn't want to waste time introducing her around. He finally had his dream girl in his arms and he didn't want to share her.

Best of all, Jessica seemed to be having a good time. She'd suffered long enough and he wanted to help her get beyond her loss, to erase the empty, faroff look in her eye. He had seen that expression in Dallas, too, but he figured with time, and understanding, it would fade. He'd wait however long it took. The lady was worth it.

"Want to sit one out?" he asked her when the song they'd been dancing to ended.

Jessica pushed a hank of hair behind her ear and shifted her weight from one foot to the other. "Yes, I think my feet could use a breather." She looked down at her black kid heels and grimaced. "I should have worn the shoes Chloe made for me. They are a lot dressier, but they fit better."

He grinned and they headed for their table, holding hands. Wiley liked having an excuse to touch her, to keep the connection. This was the way he'd pictured it would be once she moved to Red Rock—dinner at the Cowboy Club, a little dancing, and then... He gave her hand a squeeze and sighed, knowing it was the "and then" he'd been mostly waiting for. Longing for.

Damn but it had been hard to be away from her the past few weeks. He'd gotten a taste of this woman in Dallas, enough to put his brand on her, and waiting to be with her again had been hell. That little cowboy had turned their lives upside down and put things on hold, but he had a feeling his luck had changed. Jessica seemed as interested in being with him as he was with her.

Wiley let go of her hand as Jessica slid into the booth. He sat next to her, as close as he dared without looking too obvious. He still had some beer in his glass. He drained it. Jessica sipped her iced tea. They both glanced around at the lively crowd, so different from the fancy restaurant he'd taken her to in Dallas.

"Nero's seems about as far from this as Italy," he said. "Hope this isn't too down-home for you."

She gave him a wistful smile. "Ah. So, you've been recalling that night, too."

"Sugar, I've been thinking about nothing else for six weeks."

She nodded. "Me, too."

He reached over and took her hand. "This is the way it was supposed to be."

She nodded once more, but he saw that faroff look in her eye anyway. Wiley gave her hand a squeeze and she came back. Almost. He searched her eyes and saw a trace of doubt in there.

"Jessica, do we need to talk about anything?" he asked.

"Tell me your plans for the rest of the evening," she invited.

"To be honest, honey, I was wondering if I should try and entice you to go back to the ranch with me, or just tie you up and take you there, whether you're inclined to go or not."

She cocked an eyebrow. "It takes a confident man to signal his punches that way."

"Or one who knows what he wants," he said, lifting her hand to his lips and kissing her fingers.

She took his hand in both of hers, giving it a firm squeeze.

"I'd say you've had plenty of time to rest," Wiley said,

noticing the tempo of the music change. "How about dancing to a nice slow ballad?"

The prospect clearly pleased her and they returned to the dance floor. Jessica melted into his arms, her body warm and fragrant with perfume. Savoring her scent and the feel of her so close to him, Wiley knew this was what he wanted, what he'd been searching for, for years.

Sure, he was old enough to be skeptical when it came to matters of the heart, but something about Jessica Kilmer was different. He'd felt it from the moment he'd laid eyes on her, and their time in Dallas had proved it to him. All he needed now was to convince her what he already knew—that they belonged together.

THEY DIDN'T KISS until they climbed back in his truck, and when their lips finally met, Jessica realized that this was what she'd wanted from the moment they stepped onto the dance floor. In his arms, she'd felt the excitement of Dallas all over again. Yet niggling at the back of her mind, there was something else—something she couldn't quite shake. This time it wasn't the loss of her husband and child. It was that little cowboy she'd left with Ruthie Thompson.

Nathaniel had played at the edge of her thoughts all evening, often in connection with Wiley. As sexy, considerate and intelligent as the man was, she'd come to realize he was not perfect. He had a problem with kids and didn't really want them in his life—he'd said so in Dallas. And that had been fine with her, considering what she'd gone through. At least, it had been fine until a few days ago.

Sitting in Wiley's truck, as he was holding her in his arms, it hit her plain as day—caring for Nathaniel had opened her eyes to the fact that losing her daughter did not mean there wasn't room in her heart to love another child. Unfortunately, she didn't think that was true of Wiley. His loss had put him off children for good.

"So, how about I show you the Double C?" he asked, rolling a tendril of her hair around his finger. "It's beautiful country, especially on a moonlit night."

Jessica was tempted. She'd seen enough of Wiley to know that he was a man she could grow to love, deeply and completely. In a way, though, that made things worse. The last thing she needed was to fall in love with a man she wouldn't marry.

"This is one instance when no response is not a good sign," he said, interrupting her thoughts. "Am I jumping the gun?"

Jessica put her hand on his knee. "I care for you very much, and I do want to be with you, Wiley...."

"But..."

She tried to decide how to put it. "I guess I'm feeling a little distracted."

Wiley thought for a moment or two. "You're worried about Nathaniel."

She turned to him, heartened by his awareness. "Yes. Does that make me a terrible bore?"

He smiled warmly, brushing her cheek with his finger. "No," he said, "not at all. You're good-hearted and responsible. That's to be admired."

Jessica was encouraged. She didn't see any regret in his eyes, or resentment. To the contrary, he seemed to accept her feelings, if not actually approve of them. Relief washed over her.

She beamed. "I'm so glad you understand," she said, grasping his hand. They looked into each other's eyes for several moments before she spoke again. Then, "Wiley, would it be terrible of me to suggest that we swing by Mrs. Thompson's place on the way to the ranch?"

"You want to go to Ruthie's?"

"Yes. If the lights are out, I won't disturb them, of

course. But I would like to at least drive by, if that's all right. It wouldn't be too much out of the way, would it?''

Wiley chuckled. "Sweetheart, it wouldn't be out of the way at all.''

Turning the key in the ignition, he started the engine. Jessica leaned over and kissed her cowboy on the cheek.

WILEY WASN'T QUITE SURE what to make of her attachment to Sally Anne's baby. It was obvious Nathaniel was filling an emotional gap, and that wasn't a bad thing, so long as Jessica was able to keep things in perspective. But he worried what would happen if she lost sight of the fact that her involvement was only temporary.

Of course, he wasn't about to remind her of that. She was an adult. Besides, he had no right. Sure, he cared, but it was her life.

"You know one of the things I like best about you, Wiley?" she said as he turned onto Ruthie's street. "You're a very perceptive, understanding man.''

The compliment pleased him. "Comes with age and caring about the lady in question, I suppose. But thanks for saying that.''

"I appreciate that you don't try to deny me my need to care. That's generous because I realize kids are a... problem for you. A lot of men aren't up to that kind of selflessness.''

"Kids aren't so much a problem as you are a concern," he said.

"Why?"

They pulled up in front of the bungalow where Nathaniel was staying. Seeing there were lights in the front windows, Wiley turned off the engine.

"I just want you to be happy, Jessica. I want moving to Red Rock to be positive, and I want to play a part in making this the right choice.''

She caressed his cheek. "If I tell you how large a part

you played in my decision to move here, you might get a big head, so I'm not going to tell you."

Wiley grinned. "Shall we go inside and see what young Master Springer is up to?"

They got out of the truck and walked to the door. Wiley rapped lightly on the windowpane. Moments later, Ruthie lifted the corner of the blind and peered out. Then she opened the door, pulling the collar of her bathrobe closed at her neck.

"What's up?" she asked cheerfully. "Homesick already for the sounds of a crying baby?"

"We thought we'd just check to make sure everything was all right and that you didn't need anything," Jessica said.

Fussy-baby sounds were coming from the back room and Ruthie half turned to draw their attention to it. "He woke up crying about half an hour ago. I changed his diaper, but he's not quite sure that's enough attention and he's being temperamental while he tries to decide." She smiled at them. "Want to come in and say hello?"

"Would you mind?" Jessica said eagerly.

Ruthie stifled a yawn. "I'm sure the little tyke would be tickled pink to see you, honey."

She stepped back and they went inside. Nathaniel let out a cry of annoyance. Jessica shot Wiley a glance. It wasn't so much a look of concern as it was one of relief. A mother, he was beginning to see, was more concerned about what she wasn't aware of than what she was.

"You folks make yourselves at home and I'll let Nathaniel know he's got callers," Ruthie said as she headed for the back of the house.

Wiley dropped into an easy chair and Jessica sat on the edge of the sofa, her ears tuned to what was going on in back. Moments later, Ruthie returned with a cranky baby in her arms. She handed him over to Jessica without ceremony.

Nathaniel wasn't immediately impressed, continuing to fuss and cry irritably. But Jessica cooed at him and kissed him on top of the head, first getting his attention, then silencing him. Wiley watched closely, seeing something passing between the woman and the baby that looked to him an awful lot like love.

"So, how was the dancin'?" Ruthie asked.

"We had fun," Jessica said, glancing up.

Wiley nodded his agreement. "Yeah, we had a good time."

"You two make such a nice couple," Ruthie said, "if you don't mind me saying so."

"Wiley's a great dancer," Jessica said. She was looking at Nathaniel as she said it, making kissing sounds.

"That's the rumor," Ruthie replied.

Jessica did look up then, glancing in his direction. "A man with a reputation that spans all of western Colorado, I bet."

"There're a few folks down at the Cowboy Club who know I enjoy dancing," Wiley said. "The rest is gross exaggeration."

"Sure do like modesty in a man," Ruthie said, giving Jessica a wink. "Listen, can I offer you two a cup of coffee? It'll only take a minute to put a pot on."

"No, thanks," Jessica said. "We only wanted to pop in for a moment. I know we're keeping you from your sleep."

"I sort of planned on not getting too much tonight," Ruthie said, "considering my houseguest."

Nathaniel, Wiley noticed, had quieted down. "You must have been what the doctor ordered," he said to Jessica.

"He was tired and running out of steam," she said softly. "His eyelids are drooping."

"Fine by me if he wants to sleep," Ruthie said.

Jessica gave Wiley a smile and he could see bringing

her here had been the right thing to do. Yet he couldn't set aside his worries. At some level, Jessica had to realize that getting too attached to Nathaniel would only make it harder for her later. Did she know where to draw the line?

"Why don't I put him down?" Jessica whispered to Ruthie. "I think the sandman's got him."

"Come on then, honey," the woman said. "I'll show you the way."

Jessica got up and carried Nathaniel to the back room. Wiley could hear a mild protest from the baby, followed by cooing, then silence. He was on his feet when the women returned.

"Thank you for letting us barge in this way," Jessica said to Ruthie.

"Think nothing of it. You might have gained me a half an hour's sleep."

They went to the door. Wiley stepped out first onto the porch. Jessica followed.

"Come by anytime you want," Ruthie said.

Jessica thanked her again, then said good-night. After they got into the truck, Wiley looked over at her.

"Feel better?"

"Much. Thanks for indulging me."

"Ready for some moonlight?" he asked.

"Yup."

As they drove off, Wiley felt pretty damn good. What he couldn't be sure of, though, was Jessica's true state of mind. Was this the beginning of smooth sailing or the lull before the storm?

# 12

THEY ARRIVED at the Double C Ranch with a full moon overhead, so bright Jessica could easily make out the brownish-red color of the cattle and the dusty green of the sage on the nearby hills. Wiley parked the pickup near the house, but since the night air was so nice, they decided to walk for a while before going in.

They strolled hand in hand along a road that ran between two fenced pastures. Though they'd chatted some on the drive from town out to the ranch, as they walked, they lapsed into a comfortable silence. Jessica's thoughts swung gently between Wiley and the wonderful contentment she felt when they were together, and the warm, yet lightly conflicting feelings she had for Nathaniel.

She had decided that the best thing to do would be to put the baby from her mind because she'd accomplished what she could and his future was in the hands of others now. And yet, that didn't sit quite right with her. There was a yearning deep within that tugged on her emotions. It was as though Cassandra, the baby she'd buried, wasn't gone, after all—in spirit, that is. For the longest time, the gulf left by death had cut right through Jessica's soul, leaving her feeling empty.

Two people had changed that. Wiley and Nathaniel. The thing was, having Wiley in her life was a realistic possibility. Having Nathaniel wasn't. The baby was more a reminder than anything else, a reminder of what she'd once had and might have again.

Or could she?

Jessica asked herself if she was blithely going off on some romantic fantasy that was unrealistic, if not dangerous. By opening her heart to Nathaniel, was she asking for trouble? Babies weren't pets, after all. She knew that. So why had she had such a sudden change of heart?

Maybe, she thought, it had as much to do with Wiley as it did with her. Little ones usually came along with husbands. And since meeting Wiley, she'd been slowly shifting her thinking about how she wanted to spend the rest of her life. He had made her realize that she might want a family again.

"So tell me, are you eager to start practicing law here?" Wiley asked. It was almost as though he sensed that her thinking needed a new direction.

"With the excitement over the baby, I've hardly given it any thought," she confessed. "Uncle Ford's eager for me to get up to speed, though. Now that Nathaniel's gone, I can focus on work." She made the comment easily enough, but there was a little catch in her throat as the words came out.

"Ford's been chomping at the bit for you to get here," Wiley said.

"Yes, and I've promised him a full day in the office tomorrow. He also wants to take me on the rounds to meet the judges and the members of the county bar."

"I should probably do a story on you for the paper. Folks will want to know all about the new lawyer in town. Suppose I could have an interview?"

"I'm sure that could be arranged," she said, glancing over at him with a smile.

They'd come to a small rise and Wiley led her to the fence. He leaned on the top stringer and stared out across the moonlit range. Jessica, facing him, studied his shadowed profile.

How quiet and honest the man, the life, the place, she thought. Wiley wasn't loud or flashy or assertive, but there was a power in his silence, and a strength that came from his simple decency. There weren't many men like that anymore. Which was not to say he was old-fashioned. He had a sophistication and an intelligence she liked. But above all, he was real and his boots were firmly planted on the ground.

He continued to gaze out at the landscape, his chin resting on his forearms. After a long silence, he turned to face her. "Want to hear something funny? Don't take this wrong, but since meeting you I've been thinking about my ex quite a lot."

Jessica chuckled. "Is there a right way to take a comment like that?"

"What I mean is, she's the only woman I ever made an emotional commitment to. It was an unhappy experience and it was a long time ago. The truth is, that part of me has been fenced off for years now. Until I met you."

"Sounds like there may be a compliment hidden in there somewhere, after all."

"Most definitely. Since Dallas, I've been doing a lot of soul-searching, thinking about myself and the past. I guess what I'm saying is that I made the mistake of closing myself down when my marriage fell apart. I was content to leave things that way, until you came along."

"That's very sweet of you to say."

"I didn't intend it to be as sweet so much as to let you know how important having you in my life has been."

She pulled his hand to her face and pressed it to her cheek. "The feeling's mutual, Wiley."

He beamed that smile she was growing terribly, terribly fond of. "I don't know if I mentioned this before, but Juana, my housekeeper, is deaf."

"I don't know that you did. Is there a significance?"

"To me telling you now, or the fact that she is?"

"Both."

"Well, I'm telling you now, sweetheart, because I'm

about to take you inside. And her deafness means you and I will be as good as alone. Anyway, her room's in a semidetached wing out back."

"Wiley," she said with a flirtatious smile, "sounds like you're trying to tell me you've got plans for the evening."

His grin broadened. "Would it be too revealing to say I've had plans ever since I got on that plane in Dallas?"

"Would it be too revealing to say I have, too?"

With that, Wiley bent down and grabbed her behind the legs, throwing her over his shoulder.

"Wiley!" she screamed. "What are you doing?"

He began marching toward the house.

"Wiley!"

"You're in the Wild West now, sugar," he said, laughing. "Give a man an opening like that, and things are bound to happen."

"You brute!" she shouted. "And I thought you were a gentleman!"

He began to laugh. Jessica began pummeling his back, which made him laugh even harder. Finally she went limp.

"Go ahead, have your way with me," she muttered. "I give up."

Wiley went a ways farther, then he stopped and put her down. She was a little dizzy so he had to steady her before he lifted her chin and gave her a deep, sensuous kiss.

"'Whether you're buyin' cattle or courtin' a lady, never be predictable,' my grandpappy Cyrus used to say."

"How many wives did your grandpappy have, Wiley?"

"Oh, three or four, at least."

"Wore them out, did he?"

"He was a shrewd old buckaroo," Wiley said as they continued toward the house. "Honest but clever."

Jessica realized that pretty well described Wiley. Just when she thought she knew the man, he up and showed her that maybe she didn't. That made her wonder if he might have any surprises waiting for her in his bedroom.

Minutes later, they entered the dark ranch house, a sprawling home that looked to be about fifty years old. Wiley flipped on the hall light. Jessica could see immediately that it was clean, tidy and well-maintained.

"Want the ninety-second tour?" he asked.

"Sure."

He took her to the front room first. It was sunken a step. There was a huge stone fireplace on the outside wall opposite the arched entry. The big leather sofas were plush, the decor mostly western. It was pleasant, though definitely a man's home. Jessica took a moment, running her eye over the place, thinking of changes she would make. Color was the main thing. It definitely needed color.

They circled through the dining room—the chandelier she didn't much care for, though the table and chairs were nice—to the kitchen and den. The kitchen was in need of updating, but there was plenty of space to work with. She especially liked the huge pantry. The den was nice. There was a small bar in the corner.

"Care for a sherry or some port?" he asked.

"Sherry sounds good."

Wiley poured her a glass of sherry and himself some port. He did it with such finesse that it seemed impossible he was the same man who'd slung her over his shoulder.

They went to the sunroom next. The room was filled with plants and had a Mexican feel. It was far and away the most colorful, accessorized room in the house. Wiley told her that he'd let Juana decorate it and it showed. Leaving the sunroom, they stuck their heads in his office. It was a place of work, not for show. There were a lot of files and papers out, most of the surfaces covered, but the piles were neat.

Finally, they went to the master suite. Wiley told her it had been remodeled, the bathroom updated completely. Not unexpectedly, his bedroom was the most masculine of the rooms. It was all wood, brass and leather. The room wasn't unattractive, but it definitely cried out for a woman's touch. Jessica struck her head in the bathroom. It was beautiful—large, glistening, inviting. The towels were brown. She'd have gone more with mauves, corals and gray.

"You have a lovely home," she said, taking a long sip of sherry.

"It's missing a woman's touch, I know."

"Did someone tell you that?"

"Juana, I guess, has mentioned it."

"How do you feel about that?"

Wiley gave a half shrug. "There wasn't a lot to do about it, except wait for the right woman. And if one never came along, my wood and leather would do."

"That's rather stoic, Wiley."

He grinned. "I was thinking practical."

Jessica was still at the bathroom door. Wiley went over and lit an oil lamp on the chest of drawers, then turned out the lights. Afterward, he stood near the foot of the bed. Here was the man who'd playfully thrown her over his shoulder, but he didn't seem threatening or challenging. Quietly alluring was a more apt description. She really had a hard time putting her finger on what it was about him that drew her, but whatever it was, it really resonated.

After taking a last sip of sherry, she kicked off her shoes and made her way across the thick carpeting, moving in his direction with graceful, feminine strides. When she got to him, she stopped, gazing up into his deeply shadowed eyes.

"You're about the most beautiful woman I've ever laid eyes on," he said.

She reached out, hooking his fingers with hers. Their clasped hands dangled between them. There was a growing intensity in his expression and Jessica felt a rise in the cadence of her heart.

"I've missed being with you, Wiley," she said, her voice barely above a whisper.

"Darling, it couldn't be half as much as I've missed you."

She rubbed the back of his thumb with her thumb. "Think we can trust what we're feeling?"

"Trust it to be real?"

"Trust it to mean something."

"Jessica, what I feel for you goes way beyond desire."

"Is that true?"

"It's true."

She moved into his arms. She was so ready that her body responded immediately. His kiss was eager, hard, masculine. Right now she craved his strength as much as he seemed to crave her softness. Their passion deepened.

When the kiss ended, she took a deep breath, futilely trying to quiet her raging heart. She could feel the fire in her cheeks and saw the passion in his eyes. Wiley began unbuttoning her blouse. She closed her eyes, letting her head fall back. She felt him kiss her throat. Then, after slipping off her blouse, he kissed the tops of her shoulders, too.

Putting her arms around his waist, she held him close for a long moment before she finished undressing and got into the bed. As Jessica pulled the sheet over her breasts, she watched Wiley unbutton his shirt. She stared at him, mesmerized. He seemed to be all hard planes, muscle and bone. Shadow and the flickering light from the glass oil lamp played over his features. And there was something about his character, his strength, that she wanted to make a part of herself—even if it could only last as long as their lovemaking.

By the time he joined her on the bed, Wiley was already erect, his skin hot to the touch. She cuddled in his arms, kissing the span of his furry chest. He felt so right.

Wiley must have felt it, too. In spite of obviously wanting her, he took his time, caressing her slowly, playing with her as if they had an eternity to make love. His palms held her buttocks, rubbed her lower back, then gently turned her over so that he could kiss the back of her neck and each bump of her spine.

Jessica shivered with desire as each caress lingered just a little longer than the one before. When he got to her waist, she felt his tongue flick over her skin for the first time. The sensation was so electric that she felt herself moisten. And yet, as much as she wanted Wiley inside her, a lethargy overcame her. Each caress seemed to divide time into fractions of seconds that lasted longer than minutes. It was almost as if the world was slowly grinding to a halt.

By the time Wiley gave her the final kiss on her back and turned her over, Jessica knew that this would be different from any time she'd ever made love before. In Dallas, it had been good between them, but emotional—emotional in a different way. This was as if the moment they had both waited for their entire lives had finally arrived.

She looked into Wiley's eyes and he raised himself over her, a lock of hair falling across his forehead. "Are you ready for me, sweetheart?" he asked.

She opened her legs and arched her back, signaling that she wanted him inside her. He reached down between them and caressed her long enough to see that she was slick with desire. Then he entered her.

The sensation was so poignant that she wanted to cry. The emotion—the feeling of completeness—was so intense that she didn't want to move. If they could always be like this, she thought, poised on the moment when it was still all before them, it would be perfect.

But need overcame her. She began to move ever so slightly. Wiley must have understood exactly what she wanted because he started to thrust then, moving slowly, taking his time to let the desire build. Twice she was at the point of coming when he stopped thrusting to give her a chance to control herself. Each time, her desire seemed to build until she was at the point where she felt as if she could not take another moment of pleasure.

"Please, Wiley, please," she begged then.

He thrust twice more and then they both came, shuddering with desire, totally depleted. Afterward, they lay side by side for a long time in contented silence. Jessica was aware of the rise and fall of his chest. Wiley, she could tell, was lost in the aftermath of his pleasure. But he held her hand, letting her know that he was still attuned to her. Her body continued to tingle. She'd never quite known this feeling before, not even with Geoff. Here, with Wiley, seemed to be right where she belonged.

"I like this," he said softly. "I like being with you like this."

Jessica moaned her concurrence. She liked it, too, so very much. A peacefulness came over them and they began drifting toward sleep together—a rich, warm, contented sleep.

Suddenly she heard the baby cry, the sound yanking her back from the precipice of unconsciousness. She sat bolt upright, making Wiley flinch.

"Jessica?"

But then she realized the sound couldn't have been the baby. Not Cassandra, not Nathaniel. She was in Wiley's house, Wiley's bed. She heard the cry again, in the distance.

"What's that?"

"One of the cats," Wiley said.

"Oh." She dropped back down onto the bed, sighing deeply.

"Did it scare you?" he asked.

"No."

He waited for her to say more, to offer an explanation. She kept her silence for a while, then she said, "I thought it was a baby."

Wiley rolled onto his side. He stroked her hair. He kissed her shoulder tip. He understood. It made her cry.

# 13

JESSICA AWOKE SLOWLY. She didn't open her eyes, but she was aware of Wiley beside her. She snuggled a bit closer, enjoying his warmth. She eased her leg next to his, moving carefully so as not to wake him, and rubbed the top of his foot with her toes. Sighing with contentment, she thought how natural this felt, how right.

This was another timeless moment like the one she'd experienced under the weeping willow tree in Dallas. She could lie next to Wiley, savoring her wonderful memories of their night together without having to get up and face the world. She could luxuriate in the moment.

Why, she wondered, couldn't life always be like this? Instead of rushing around from one crisis to the next, why couldn't you slow down and treasure each experience for what it offered? Was that an unrealistic goal?

She realized it probably was. Life didn't work that way. Yet, with planning and a little cooperation from the right partner, there could be many times like this... times when being alone together was enough to give a sense of peace and completion.

Wiley reached over and took her hand. "I don't want to wake up, either," he said, his voice barely above a whisper.

Jessica smiled, though she still didn't open her eyes. "How long have you been awake?"

"Long enough to know that I'd like to stay like this for about a thousand years."

She gave his fingers a squeeze. "Is that all?"

"Well, by then I might be hungry. Speaking of which, would you like to have some of Juana's buttermilk pancakes for breakfast, or a waffle?"

Jessica opened her eyes and sat bolt upright. Lord, she'd forgotten all about the housekeeper. She'd forgotten about work...everything. "What time is it?"

Wiley pulled away from her to look at the clock on the bedstand on his side of the bed. "Just after six."

Jessica hopped out of bed and began picking her clothes off the floor. "I have to get out of here before your housekeeper sees me."

"Juana doesn't care if you're here."

"Well, I care."

He rubbed his eyes and stretched. "You're serious, aren't you?"

"I've got my pride," she replied.

"Remind me to fire Juana," he groused.

"Don't be difficult. I've got to get into town, change my clothes, show up at the office... You get the picture."

"Okay, sweetheart, whatever makes you happy."

She had a quick shower, but didn't bother to wash her hair. Wiley wanted to make some coffee for them before they left, but she wouldn't let him. As they climbed into his truck, the first glow of light shone behind the mountains to the east.

"Thanks for indulging me," she said, touching his arm. "I know this is a pain."

"But well worth it," he said, giving her chin a pinch.

As they headed into town, she looked out at the tumbleweed piled up behind a barbed-wire fence and sighed heavily. Their night had been wonderful. But now that it was a new day, she had a nagging feeling something was wrong. Almost as if something was missing. But what?

"You're being mighty quiet," he said.

"Don't mean to be."

"Everything all right? Was there anything about last night that..."

"Last night was perfect."

"Really perfect?"

"You're a wonderful lover, Wiley. You made me very happy."

"But..."

She glanced over at him. "It's nothing."

"You might as well share."

"The past isn't easily forgotten."

He didn't comment immediately, driving for a while in silence. Then he said, "Are we really talking about the past, Jessica?"

"No. Not entirely. But the past and the present are kind of tied together, aren't they?"

"Is it Nathaniel?"

She sighed. "I suppose I got a bit more emotionally involved than I should have."

"That's okay as long as you realize it's a mistake."

She blinked. "What do you mean, a mistake?"

"His situation will all be resolved sooner or later, probably when Sally Anne is found, or comes to her senses."

Jessica was stunned. His comment sounded almost...heartless. Maybe what he said was true, but did he have to put it so bluntly? Anyway, how could Wiley be so sure? "You sound like that's what you want," she said.

"Well, sure. Isn't that in everybody's best interest?"

Jessica saw there was no point in arguing. She'd only get emotional and, besides, no one knew with certainty what would happen. Given that, it'd be stupid to create hard feelings. But it was too bad Wiley hadn't come to that conclusion himself before he opened his mouth.

They lapsed into silence. Wiley must have realized

he'd hurt her feelings because he started making concil-
iatory sounds.

"If you're concerned about the way things are being
handled, why don't you get yourself appointed as Nathaniel's lawyer?"

She looked at him.

"Seriously," Wiley said. "There's a legal term for that.
It came up when I was getting my divorce."

"You mean *guardian ad litem?*"

"Yeah, that's it."

"You don't necessarily have to be a lawyer for that."

"Couldn't hurt. You'd know what you're doing."

"And why would I want to?" she asked, crossing her
arms over her chest.

"It'd be a good way for you to look out for Nathaniel's interests. You obviously care about him. Court-
appointed guardian would be a better role for you than
baby-sitter. Leave the day-to-day care to Ruthie Thompson."

Jessica wondered if that was Wiley's way of saying she
should deny her feelings by thinking and acting like a
lawyer...instead of a woman. But why argue about it?
She knew he probably meant well. Wiley wasn't callous,
but he was a man, and men tended to think everything
could be solved by logic.

By the time they reached the outskirts of Red Rock, the
sun was peeking over the mountains. Wiley drove directly to her house. Jessica felt shaky enough that she
didn't want to be near him. What she needed, she figured, was solitude so she could think this thing through.
But when Wiley brought the truck to a stop and looked
over at her with his crinkly blue eyes, he once again
seemed the caring, good-hearted cowboy who made her
heart flutter. Unfortunately, he simply didn't understand
she couldn't reason herself out of the dilemma she was
in.

"Our predicament is only temporary," he said, taking her hand. "Everything's going to work out, I'm sure."

"Yes, I know," she said. "You're right." She leaned over and kissed him on the lips. "Last night was wonderful. Thank you."

"Have plans for dinner?"

"I've got a day's work ahead of me with Uncle Ford. And, frankly, I need a good night's sleep. Between you and Nathaniel, it's been a while since I've had eight hours."

"How about if I call you later, then?"

"Okay, great."

Jessica got out of the truck and hurried up to her front door. Once inside, she felt the threat of tears again, but she resisted it. Wiley was right about one thing—she needed to be constructive. Maybe he had hit the nail on the head when he'd suggested that she should approach this problem as a lawyer. That was what she was trained for, after all. Besides, if she tackled the situation with both her head and her heart, she might be able to come up with a solution she could live with.

WHEN JESSICA ARRIVED at her uncle's office, he greeted her as if she were the prodigal son. She'd been neglecting him since her arrival, though it wasn't entirely her doing. Ford had acknowledged being as much a party to saddling her with the baby problem as anyone else. But the time had come to get down to business.

First, Ford showed her the office he'd readied for her. It was small but pleasant. Once she fixed it up, it would be downright homey. The big wooden desk was nice. On her desk in Dallas, she'd had photos of Cassandra and Geoff. It no longer seemed appropriate to have a picture of Geoff on her desk, but could she have one without the other?

Before lunch, Ford wanted to go over the active cases

in the office, so the two of them sat in the small conference room and reviewed Ford's files. The diversity of his cases was more impressive than the number, which was considerable. It was no surprise he felt he needed help.

"There are only eleven of us practicing in the county," Ford said, "and two of the eleven are semiretired. I won't be the only one welcoming new blood."

"I'm looking forward to it."

"I thought maybe we could have dinner in Cortez. I'll round up as many of the boys as I can so you can get acquainted with everybody."

"I'd like that."

The mention of Cortez made her think about the social worker who was scheduled to visit Ruthie Thompson this morning. Jessica wondered how that had gone. She checked her watch. It was shortly before noon. Off and on during the morning, she'd thought of Ruthie and the baby, hoping that their night had been all right. Several times she'd started to pick up the phone, but had stopped herself. Constantly checking up on Nathaniel was no way to put emotional distance between them, which would be necessary if she wanted to look at the situation from the point of view of a lawyer. But she saw no harm in seeing how the interview went.

Ford had mumbled something about them wandering over to the Cowboy Club for lunch, but Jessica knew she'd enjoy the experience more if she talked to Ruthie first. "I need to make a phone call before we leave," she told her uncle.

"Fine. I'll make a few calls to Cortez to firm up things for dinner tonight."

They each went to their office. Ruthie Thompson sounded glad Jessica had phoned.

"No problems with Nathaniel last night," she said. "He mostly slept through and had a nice breakfast this morning. But I'm afraid the county wants to take him."

"What do you mean?"

"Ivy Dix, the social worker, called first thing this morning and said there was no point in her driving all the way over here only to turn around and come back tomorrow or the day after to pick him up. She asked if I had a problem with her taking Nathaniel now."

"What did you say?"

"That I didn't mind personally, but Mr. Lewis might, since he was the one who arranged for Nathaniel to stay with me."

"And she said…"

"Basically, if Mr. Lewis had a problem with it, he could talk to Judge Whitaker."

Jessica felt her blood begin to boil. "When is this woman, Ivy Dix, coming?"

"In about half an hour."

"Ruthie, would you mind if I dropped by and had a word with Ms. Dix?"

"No, the less I have to talk to her the better."

"I'll be there as soon as I can."

Jessica ended the call and went to Ford's office. She explained what had happened.

"Damn bureaucrats," he said. "I'll put in another call to the county."

"Before you do, let me ask you something. How do you think Judge Whitaker would react to a *guardian ad litem* petition for Nathaniel?"

"In favor of who? Wiley?"

"No, me."

"You? Guardian for the baby?"

"*Guardian ad litem.* Just to look out for his interests."

Ford stroked his chin, his forehead creased. "Why in tarnation would you—"

"I have my reasons. But I need to know how the judge would likely respond."

Her uncle shook his head. "Your first question and

you've got me stumped. I don't imagine there's been three petitions for an *ad litem* in this county in the past hundred years, if that." He pondered for a moment. "I expect Judge Whitaker would say the same thing I did. What for?"

"I believe I can make a persuasive case."

"Well, have at it, if that's what you've set your mind to."

"How soon could I get a hearing?"

Ford checked his watch. "If the docket's not too full and there's not a big trial in progress, an hour's notice is possible. But it's already a little late for today. Call now and you could probably get on for tomorrow morning."

She turned on her heel.

"Jessica," Ford called, stopping her.

"Yes?"

"Have you given this serious thought?"

"More than Judge Whitaker will, I'm sure."

IVY DIX, a tall, bony woman with the scowl of a cranky librarian, was already at Ruthie's place when Jessica arrived. Introductions were made.

Ivy did not strike Jessica as a bad person—actually, she was probably caring and dedicated. But she was pushing toward retirement and it was not surprising she'd want to avoid the drive back to Red Rock from the county offices if she could avoid it. Jessica explained her intentions, saying she'd arranged a hearing in Judge Whitaker's courtroom for nine the next morning.

"Let me ask you this, Miss Kilmer," Ivy Dix said. "What if Judge Whitaker denies your motion?"

"Then I guess I'll have to bring Nathaniel to Cortez."

"Seems like it would be a lot easier if I take him now," the woman grumbled. "You're still going to have to find a foster home and Mrs. Thompson's said she only planned on keeping the baby for a couple of days."

"That'll be my problem."

"I beg to differ, Miss Kilmer," Ivy said. "Until Nathaniel Springer is placed for adoption or returned to his natural parents, he's a ward of the state. If you're appointed to represent him in court, that doesn't mean the county's responsibility ends."

"The judge can decide, and I'll have some recommendations."

"So will I."

Jessica smiled, biting her tongue to keep from saying, "See you in court." Instead, she said, "I'm sure we can work things out to everyone's satisfaction."

After a curt goodbye, the county social worker left. Ruthie shook her head.

"What could possibly make that woman think she's able to protect anyone? I'll bet she couldn't pet a dog without getting bit."

"She does everything by the numbers," Jessica said. "She is right about one thing—we have to figure out what we're going to do with Nathaniel."

"I'd love to help," Ruthie said, "but I can't keep a baby long-term. A few nights is all I promised Mr. Lewis."

"I understand. But don't worry, I'll get to work on it right away."

There was a cry of protest from the back room. Jessica's heart gave a lurch. Nathaniel was sleeping when she'd arrived and he'd been the absent subject of the discussion.

"Somebody's getting hungry," Ruthie said.

Jessica realized this would be a good time to make her exit. The less she saw of Nathaniel, the easier it would be. Keeping her distance was the key. Besides, Ford was waiting for her at the Cowboy Club, and they had to drive over to the county seat.

"Want to say hello to the little rascal?" Ruthie asked as the baby let out another squawk.

Jessica started to say no, but Ruthie had given her an excuse and the temptation was simply too great. "Okay, sure."

They went into the back room. Nathaniel was in a crib. "Where did that come from?" Jessica asked.

"Kate MacInnes sent it over along with a bunch of clothes and things. And two women from the community church came by with toys and some baby food."

Jessica moved closer to the crib, touched by the thought that there were so many people who genuinely cared about this child. The town of Red Rock was assuming the responsibility, which showed that it did take more than just a mother and father to raise a child. Nathaniel looked up at her. Was there recognition on his face, or was it wishful thinking?

Unable to help herself, Jessica scooped him into her arms and held him to her breast, kissing the top of his fuzzy little head. Ruthie beamed.

"Maybe you should take him yourself," the woman said, "at least until they find his mother or he's put up for adoption."

Jessica looked over at her, recalling that the woman's words echoed Wiley's and wondering if Ruthie had been talking to him. Then she realized that it was only common sense that one or the other outcome would happen eventually. Oh, it was possible he'd be in foster care until he was of age, but she doubted it. Somebody in Red Rock would want to keep him. Or, if not here, then certainly elsewhere. But that was not her immediate problem.

"Can you give me one more night, Ruthie? I'll find a place for him by tomorrow."

"Sure. I was planning on it."

Giving Nathaniel a little kiss goodbye, Jessica handed him to the woman and made a quick exit before the farewell got any more difficult.

THE NEXT MORNING, Jessica sat in Judge Arnold Whitaker's courtroom, waiting for her petition to be heard. She'd drafted it the night before, after she and Ford had gotten back from their dinner in Cortez. Eight of the eleven lawyers in the county had been at the dinner. Judge Whitaker and Judge Peeler had both put in appearances and Jessica was glad because it was best to know a judge before you had to plead before him or her. She and Judge Whitaker had chatted for a few minutes, but they hadn't discussed her petition. As he was leaving, though, he said, "Understand we have an appointment in the morning."

She'd smiled and told him, "Yes," and that she was looking forward to it. But now that the moment had arrived, she was as nervous as the first time she'd gone to court after passing the bar and getting sworn in. Since she'd returned to Colorado, this would be her "first time out of the chute," as Ford had described it. And there was a lot at stake.

On the way home the previous evening, her uncle had told her enough about Judge Whitaker for Jessica to know the man could be daunting. "Arnold's fair, but he can be gruff. And he's getting to that cranky age."

"You're making it sound like appearing before him is an ordeal."

"Picture a rodeo cowboy in judicial robes," Ford said. "Because that's exactly what Arnold is."

Jessica had to admit the judge had the leathery look of a cowboy, but it was soon apparent he ran a tight ship. When the case was called, the judge asked her to approach the bench.

"I've looked over your petition, Ms. Kilmer, and everything seems to be in order. But I'd like you to explain why it's necessary. Don't you think the county people can look out for a nine-month-old baby without having a lawyer peering over their shoulder?"

Jessica could see she was going to be in for a rough time. "I'm sure the county officials are fully competent, Your Honor," she replied. "But we have a case of a child being abandoned by a mother who is herself a minor. She will quite possibly be facing criminal charges. Her legal representative will be focused on her problems, leaving neither the mother nor her counsel at liberty to devote their full attention to the welfare of the child. A *guardian ad litem* will bring an objectivity to a process that will be adversarial for reasons having nothing to do with the child's welfare."

Judge Whitaker pondered her comment. "Okay," he said, his gruff voice echoing throughout the room. "Assuming that's true, why you? Granted, you're admitted to practice law before this court, but you're new to the community."

"I submit that would make me an even better advocate, Your Honor. I do not know the child's mother, nor most of the other personalities who are likely to be involved. I have an objectivity that should serve the interests of the minor child concerned."

The judge rubbed his large hand across his lips to hide the smile that had formed. "Well, I can't see any harm in what you propose so long as you aren't asking that public resources be committed to your efforts."

"No, Your Honor. I'm offering my services pro bono."

"I reckon even a nine-month-old baby can afford free representation." Reaching for his gavel, he added, "Petition granted. Thank you, Miss Kilmer." He turned to his clerk. "Next case."

Jessica's heart soared. "Thank you, Judge Whitaker."

The judge frowned. "All your appearances before this court won't necessarily be this smooth, Counselor," he said. "But every lawyer's entitled to a honeymoon, however brief." He motioned for her to go.

Jessica left the courthouse on cloud nine. Now all she had to do was figure out how she was going to take care of Nathaniel. She checked her watch, realizing that she had until tomorrow morning to find him a foster home.

# 14

YOU'RE WHAT?" Ford said the next morning. He'd just gotten back from an early-morning meeting with Julia Sommers at the Lone Eagle Ranch. Now he was back in his law office.

"I'm going to request custody myself," Jessica repeated.

"That's what I thought you said. Lord, I know it's a question I've been asking a lot, but why? Why in tarnation would you want to do that?"

"Because I can't find anybody else to do it. I spent two hours with Jamie Cole last night. She must have made thirty calls. We found two good prospects but neither couple could take immediate custody. And since whoever we got would have to be approved to provide foster care, we decided it might as well be me."

"Even if the judge agrees with you, is it a good idea? Really?"

"Why not?"

"Well, for starters, how are you going to practice law and look after a baby?"

"Jamie and I worked out a deal with Ruthie Thompson and her friend Liz Chromer. They'll split day-care duties. That way, neither of them will get overworked. I'll look after Nathaniel evenings and weekends."

Ford leaned back in his big, maroon leather desk chair. "This won't do wonders for your social life, you know," he said.

She gave him a look. "Since when are you concerned with my social life, Uncle Ford?"

"Well, I know somebody who is."

"I'm having lunch with Wiley. I'm going to tell him, then."

Her uncle pondered the situation. "There's no guarantee the county people will approve you as a foster parent. A single working woman, who has to hire babysitters. I may be an old bachelor, but I think it's a safe bet when I say that's probably not what they have in mind."

"Single women adopt children all the time, for heaven's sake."

"Yes, but foster parenting is state care. When I talked to the county for you, I asked why there were so few approved foster parents. They said it was because the standards are so rigorous."

"Then I guess you're going to have to pull a few strings, Uncle Ford."

"Hey, young lady, I may have a few markers out, but at the rate you're going, I'll owe everybody in the county."

She gave him her sweetest smile. "It's for a good cause."

"I'll need an argument," he said flatly. "Something to hang my hat on."

Jessica thought for a moment. "Tell them I'm thinking seriously of adopting him."

Ford's mouth sagged open.

She shrugged. "It's an argument."

Her uncle stroked his jaw as he studied her. "Honey, are you sure you aren't getting into dangerous waters?"

"What do you mean?"

"Aren't you kind of emotionally vulnerable right now? You could be opening yourself up to more pain and disappointment."

"Uncle Ford, Nathaniel needs me."

The expression on his face said he thought she was grasping at straws. Jessica's fear was that he might be right.

"YOU'RE WHAT?" Wiley said when she told him.

Jessica rolled her eyes. "Those words must be part of the Y chromosome. Uncle Ford said the same thing."

He gave a little laugh. "You're kidding, right?"

"No, I'm not kidding," she said with a frown. "It's the only reasonable solution."

They were in the Cowboy Club, their menus in front of them. Wanda, who was helping to serve the drinks because they were shorthanded, brought them their iced tea.

"You kids want to order?"

"Sure," Wiley said. "I'll have the tostada salad."

Wanda turned to her. "The same," Jessica said.

After the hostess left, Wiley looked at her. Jessica wasn't happy to see that he was frowning again. "Forgive me for saying this, but I fail to see what's reasonable about you taking on full-time responsibility for a baby. You're only setting yourself up to get hurt."

She grimaced. "Did you talk to Ford before you came over here? Because you keep saying the same things."

"Maybe because our line of reasoning is so obvious."

"What's so obvious about it?" she said, getting annoyed. "That I couldn't possibly know what I'm doing? What makes you and Ford the authorities on what's good for me? Answer me that, Wiley Cooper!"

He regarded her in silence, though his mouth was in a tight line. Jessica realized she'd overreacted.

"I'm sorry, Wiley. I didn't mean to snap. It's just that I really don't understand why this is such a bad idea. There's a helpless baby in need."

"True. But you aren't the only person in the world willing to help. There are other resources."

"Is that really it? Or is the idea of my being involved with a baby uncomfortable for you?"

He thought for a moment before answering. When he finally spoke, his tone was low and even. "I'd like to think my concern is for you. My impression was that dealing with Nathaniel wasn't an easy thing for you…emotionally, I mean."

She sighed. "I understand how you came to that conclusion. Actually, I've come to realize that Nathaniel is good for me. I was hiding from my pain to keep from confronting it. That's why I couldn't seem to heal. Having this experience has helped me face that. I can't spend my life running from the sight of a baby. The sooner I deal with my loss, and get on with my life, the better."

He took a deep breath and exhaled slowly. "If you're being helped, then I'm glad. I truly am."

The words were generous, but she could sense there was more. Something he hadn't said. "But what? What is it you aren't saying?"

He shook his head, obviously not wanting to answer the question.

"Come on. Tell me."

Wiley took another long breath. "I kind of thought maybe you and I were building a relationship, Jessica."

She froze, realizing she'd been right after all. His primary concern *was* about him. He wasn't into children and he saw her feelings for Nathaniel as threatening. Considering what he'd been through, she could understand that. She reached out and took his hands.

"My feelings for you haven't changed, Wiley. This doesn't have anything to do with us. It's something *I* need to work through for *me*. Nathaniel is like therapy. Besides, the arrangement is only temporary, until his status is clarified. I figure, why send him over to some foster home, when I'm fully capable, and when having him will be good for my soul?"

"You're saying you can take care of him, love him, and then just turn him over to someone else when the time comes?"

She hesitated. "Yes. I guess that's what I am saying."

His expression was skeptical. "Well, I hope you don't get hurt." He took a sip of tea. "And I hope you won't hold it against me that I intend to keep on trying to track down Sally Anne. I want to find a solution that's in both her interest and Nathaniel's."

"No, I realize you feel an obligation because of Lucas."

"Do you see that this puts us on opposite sides, in a sense?"

"Perhaps. But let's not forget that we both want what's best for the baby."

He did not seem convinced. "I sure hope you're right."

She took his hands again, squeezing them. "You and I are a separate issue, entirely."

He nodded, but she could see he still had doubts. Worse, it was obvious that in solving one problem, she'd created another—maybe one that was even bigger.

JESSICA TRIED not to worry about their relationship, though that wasn't easy. Clearly, this was a test—a big test. And she wasn't sure whether or not they could manage to bridge the gap that had formed between them. She'd been married to Geoff long enough to know that it took more than good intentions. Both people had to want to make things work.

Even though in her heart of hearts she wanted Wiley in her life, she knew that this test wasn't all bad. In fact, at a subconscious level, she might even have wanted this to happen. After all, if they couldn't see eye to eye on the issue of children, it was better to know it now, before they were too deeply committed. In a sense, Nathaniel was her way of getting right to the heart of the matter.

She spent the afternoon going through the office files

and catching up on various cases. But it wasn't easy to concentrate. She kept thinking of Wiley and second-guessing herself. What did she really want? If the time came when she might have to make a choice, could she commit to the man, given this apparent chasm separating them?

There had been underlying tension between them during lunch, and they had both felt it. Jessica had done what she could to ease it by inviting Wiley to dinner Saturday night. He'd responded positively. At least they hadn't fought.

Jessica noticed the phones had been ringing quite a bit, but Judy had arrived and was taking the calls. Shortly after one of the phone calls, her uncle came to her office, rapping lightly on the door frame.

"Well, you've been given the green light to look after Nathaniel," Ford said, not sounding altogether pleased. "The county just called. Ivy Dix and Judge Whitaker worked out a deal. You've been granted temporary, provisional custody."

She couldn't help a broad smile from forming on her face. "Temporary, provisional, huh? Sounds like they don't want me to get too full of myself."

"I think it's a mistake, myself, but if it's what you want…"

"Thanks, Uncle Ford, for all your effort."

"I'm no authority on children and families, Jessica, but keep your wits about you and don't let your emotions get in the way."

"Spoken like a true bachelor."

"I'm serious."

"I know you are. But this is something I need to do. I'm healing. That's important, too."

"You might want to let Ruthie Thompson know."

"I'll call her now."

He nodded and left.

Jessica got on the phone. Ruthie was pleased to hear the news because she knew how important this was to her.

"When do you want to pick the little varmint up, honey?"

"I guess right after work."

"I'll have everything ready."

Jessica tried to work, but all she could think about was Nathaniel. He wasn't a replacement for Cassandra, but in a very special way he would be her guide. He'd help open her heart.

Ford left the office early to take care of some city business. Jessica worked diligently on her files until Judy left for the day, then decided she could go, too. She'd have work to do at home, getting Nathaniel all set up.

She was stuffing some files into her briefcase, thinking she'd try to get in a little work at home, when she heard the front door open.

"Hello? Anybody here?" It was Wiley's voice.

"Just us chickens," she called as she stepped over to her office door.

Wiley was standing by Judy's desk in the outer office. He had a newspaper in his hand. "Brought the special edition by for you to see," he said. "You're featured prominently on the front page."

"Oh, really?" she said, walking to the desk.

Wiley handed her the paper. There was a large picture of her holding Nathaniel under the banner headline, Baby Left at Cowboy Club, with the subheading, Foundling has Red Rock Roots. Jessica read the first several paragraphs of the story. She was identified in the story as Mayor Lewis's niece, a new arrival in town, who, along with Ruthie Thompson, had been caring for Nathaniel Springer until other arrangements were made.

Jessica looked up at Wiley with shimmering eyes.

"Seeing it in print kind of gets to you," she murmured.

"You're the town heroine."

"If not the town fool."

"You'll be fine," Wiley said.

Jessica was so grateful for his support that she hugged him. While she was in Wiley's arms, all her warm feelings for him came flooding back, despite the problems she knew they had. That reminded her how much she was risking.

"The county has agreed to let me have temporary custody of the baby," she told him, resting her chin on his shoulder.

"Yeah, I heard."

"You don't hate me, do you, Wiley?" she said.

He pulled back so he could see her face. "Of course not. How could I?"

"This really is about me...coming to terms with my grief."

"I know," he said.

She knew he didn't really believe that.

"Well, I've got things to do," he told her. "I'd better go."

Briefly, he touched her cheek with his palm and then left the office. Jessica stood there for several moments, her heart feeling torn in two. Sometimes it seemed there was no way to win.

WHEN SHE ARRIVED at Ruthie's and found a smiling, happy baby waiting, Jessica knew that taking Nathaniel into her heart and her life couldn't be a mistake. Sure, it might be inconvenient—even unwise—but how could giving an innocent little boy a piece of her heart be wrong?

She and Ruthie loaded Nathaniel's things into the car. As Ruthie handed her a box of clothing and toys various people had brought by, she said, "How is it Wiley isn't helping you move the baby back?"

"He's pretty busy," she replied.

"I expect if he's like most men, you look a lot more attractive without a baby than with one."

"You may be right. But it's hard for a man who hasn't spent much time around kids to get used to sharing."

Ruthie probably could tell that she was making excuses for Wiley, but at the same time, Jessica knew that the man was as entitled to his feelings and sensitivities as she was to hers. Besides, he didn't owe her anything. Before she'd left Dallas, they'd agreed there was no guarantee that things would work out.

"Never can tell," Ruthie said. "He might come around. Sometimes it takes a man time gettin' used to an idea."

Jessica wasn't so sure that would work in Wiley's case. The days ahead would be revealing.

Once they had everything in the car, Jessica put Nathaniel in the car seat that Ruthie's daughter had brought by. The two women said their goodbyes, then Jessica drove home.

It was different this time taking the baby's things into the little place she now called home. First, she was alone. But the biggest difference was that she was acting with a sense of commitment. She felt Nathaniel belonged to her more than to anybody in the world, except Sally Anne, of course. They had that bond, if no other.

Once she had everything put away, Jessica brought Nathaniel into the kitchen and put him in the worn baby seat that somebody in town had donated. She wanted to watch him while she fixed their dinner. She'd done the same thing with Cassandra, finding that it made cooking and other housework more enjoyable when she could talk to her baby while she worked.

"So, what do you think, Nathaniel?" she said. "How long do you figure we've got together? You a betting man?"

The baby cooed and gurgled, waving his arms excitedly. Jessica wondered at Sally Anne, the kind of person she was. She had to have passed many anguished nights since leaving her son at the Cowboy Club. The question was, how anguished? And would she have second thoughts? Jessica knew Wiley was expecting something like that to happen, even hoping for it. Maybe the county people were, too. The words kept ringing in her head— "temporary" and "provisional."

"Well, that's okay," Jessica said to the baby. "Maybe that's all the time we need."

JUST AFTER DINNER, as she was sitting down in the living room with the baby, there was a phone call. It was Kate MacInnes.

"Great story in the paper. Wiley really outdid himself."

"He cares a lot because it's Lucas's grandchild."

"Seems to me he cares about the lady quite a bit, too," Kate said.

Jessica hoped that would still be true a month from now. "Yeah, I guess."

"I hear you've asked for custody of the baby. How did that come about?"

She told the story, placing most of the emphasis on her desire to keep Nathaniel from being shipped off to Cortez. "The other reason is, I think it's something I need to do."

"That's admirable," Kate said, "but you don't have to carry the burden alone. I know there are many townspeople who want to help. In fact, that brings me to the other reason for my call. I've been thinking that it would be nice to have a baby shower and get Nathaniel some loot, so you and Wiley won't have all the expense."

"People have been very generous already, Kate. You wouldn't believe how much stuff has been donated."

"Yeah, but most of it's pretty old. People will have to

bring real gifts if we have a shower. I'm willing to organize it."

Jessica wasn't sure how she felt about that except that it certainly was generous of Kate. But then, everyone in Red Rock had gone out of their way to be kind. "That would be nice."

"What do you think of Saturday afternoon?"

"It works for me."

"We'll have it at my house," Kate said, "if that's all right."

"Sure, great."

"I'll be back in touch with details, but right now I'd better get on the phone and start inviting people. I already ran the idea past Wanda and Julia Sommers and they were thrilled. All they're waiting for is the go-ahead from you."

"Did you happen to talk to Chloe?" Jessica asked. "I've been in town several days now, and I still haven't run into her. We really hit it off when I came here to visit a few months ago and I was sort of hoping that we'd get together again."

"Yes, I talked to her. She's been down with a sore throat. And since she just found out that she's expecting her first, she didn't want to take any chances. But she ought to be well by Saturday. Dax will probably bring her over on a satin pillow. Chloe said he was being very attentive."

Jessica laughed and they said goodbye, promising to touch base again about the time for the party. As Jessica hung up the telephone, she couldn't help reflecting on what Kate had said about Dax being so attentive. Geoff, too, had been terribly solicitous, at least at first. But what would Wiley be like? And would she ever have a chance to find out?

# 15

OVER THE NEXT FEW DAYS, Jessica began to get the feeling her decision to take in Nathaniel had been a fateful one. Though Wiley hadn't actually said anything, she felt a new distance between them that made her wonder if he thought she'd chosen the baby over him. That wasn't true, of course, though she *had* forced the issue.

And it hadn't taken her long to realize that this was kind of a test that would show what was most important to each of them. Considering his recent withdrawal from her, she realized it was also the only way she could be true to herself.

Meanwhile, Jessica's feelings for Nathaniel began to change. She no longer tried to keep herself from loving him. And when the floodgates opened, and she felt the little cowboy begin to worm his way into her heart, she let herself love again. Of course, she knew she was taking a terrible chance. There was a real possibility, even a likelihood, that Nathaniel would be taken from her at some point, maybe sooner rather than later. But she almost didn't care. By allowing herself to feel love, she was freeing herself from her pain. She was reaching out. Living again.

It had been almost the same with her love for Wiley. In allowing herself to care for him, she'd banished many of the ghosts from the past. But there'd been risk in that, and it was possible she was paying for it now. She and her cowboy were compatible in so many ways, but Nathaniel was a stumbling block. Jessica, in her roles as a woman and a mother, were at odds. Wiley wanted her, but not her baggage.

The thing was, she couldn't say he was wrong. After all, Wiley had his needs, too. It could be that they simply weren't compatible. Not deep down.

He was scheduled to come over for dinner Saturday night, but rather than looking forward to it, she was beginning to dread it—not because she didn't want to be with him, rather, it was because she sensed their differences would be coming to a head. They could only pretend so long. Even if Nathaniel was suddenly out of the picture, the issue would remain. Because if the little foundling had taught her anything, it was that she wanted to be a mother again.

On Friday, when Jessica arrived at the office, Ford told her that he had to put on his "mayor hat" and go to an emergency meeting with the county planning director. She agreed to cover his ten o'clock appointment with the Wainwrights, an elderly couple who wanted to revise their wills. "All you have to do is update the file and find out what it is they want to do now. They've had grandchildren since the last will, so I expect they want to factor them into the equation," he said, on his way out the door.

Jessica knew there would be a fair amount of this sort of thing in the coming months and that was fine because it was one of the reasons Ford had been so eager for her to join the practice. Besides, the more clients she interacted with, the better. Ford had hinted broadly that he planned to retire in not too many more years, and if she were to take over the practice completely, it was important she develop a personal relationship with as many clients as possible.

The Wainwrights, it turned out, were a delight. A sweet couple that seemed as much in love as the day they married over fifty years earlier. "At this point in life," Thelma Wainwright said as her husband held her hand, "our children and grandchildren are the most important things in the world. We want to make everything as comfortable for them as we can."

It was a heartwarming sentiment, but one that would have upset Jessica only days earlier. Coming now, instead of reminding her of her losses, it was an affirmation of her feelings. Yes, one day she'd like to be like Mrs. Wainwright, sharing her life and her feelings with a man she loved.

Jessica took down the Wainwrights' information and told them that either she or Ford would get back to them with a revised will to review. The couple thanked her and Jessica walked them to the door.

As she looked out, she saw Wiley Cooper crossing the street. Her heart gave a little jump. He was in his hat, jeans and boots...her cowboy who'd rescued her from the emotional shell she'd built around herself. But he was also the man who'd disappointed her, going from ally to cautious friend, if not adversary. Jessica hadn't thought about it from his standpoint a whole lot, but she realized now that she had probably disappointed poor Wiley every bit as much as he'd disappointed her.

She turned from the window knowing that he hadn't seen her watching him, and was looking at the files on Judy's desk when the door opened and Wiley stepped inside. She glanced up, trying to look surprised.

"Oh, hi, Wiley."

He took off his hat, nodding politely, without really smiling. There was something ominous in his eyes, which gave her pause. He shifted uneasily and cleared his throat. She grew more wary.

"I just talked to the sheriff. There's some news I thought you ought to hear."

She braced herself. "What news?"

"They found out where Sally Anne had been living the past few months. They think she left the state, but aren't sure where she was headed. Speculation is she had some help."

"Sounds like you're saying they'll likely find her."

"Usually girls in her situation turn up eventually. The fear, of course, is that she might get herself in trouble first. A kid on the road is an easy target."

"You must be worried sick," Jessica said.

"I'm concerned," he replied, lowering his eyes. Then he added, "Concerned about you as much as Sally Anne."

"Why me?"

"Well, something's bound to happen that'll upset the status quo."

She swallowed hard. "You've already warned me about getting too attached to Nathaniel."

"And I told you why—because I don't want you hurt, Jessica."

"Thanks, but I'm in this with my eyes open."

"You sure?"

She didn't know whether to insist she was fine and avoid the issue altogether, or to admit that she'd chosen to throw caution to the wind and given herself permission to love a baby that wasn't hers. She decided on the conservative approach.

"I'm okay, Wiley," she said. "I'm taking one day at a time."

He lowered his eyes again, slowly turning his hat in his hands. "I realize we have different opinions about the best way to handle this situation, but I want you to know I admire you, Jessica. You have the courage of your convictions and you truly care. And I do understand how hard this is to be in limbo." He gave her a tentative smile. "Well, I'm due at the paper. Gotta run."

He was half out the door before she could reply. But he stopped, sticking his head back inside.

"We still on for tomorrow night?" he asked.

"Yes, I've been looking forward to it."

"Me, too. See you then."

And he was gone.

That evening, Jessica picked Nathaniel up early from Ruthie's and took him home and held him for a long, long time before fixing dinner. She needed to test her feelings and her resolve.

"What do you think, kiddo? Are we making a mistake getting too friendly?"

Nathaniel looked up at her and did exactly the wrong thing, of course. He cooed at her and smiled, reaching his plump little hand toward her face. It was enough to bring tears to her eyes.

"You're no help," she muttered. "I think we'd have both been better off if you'd stayed with your mother. Of course, it wasn't exactly your choice, was it?"

Jessica had a sinking feeling, a feeling of impending doom. Even if she'd been a fool to give her love to this baby, at least she hadn't run from her desires. She'd followed her heart.

Now, of course, she'd have to face the consequences. She was determined, though, that Nathaniel wouldn't suffer because of it and, if she could avoid it, she wasn't going to let it get her down. Kate was throwing her a baby shower and Jessica was set on enjoying it, come what may.

She took the baby into the kitchen and fixed dinner, doing her best to stay cheerful and upbeat. Nathaniel did his part by being a perfect baby. Ironically, Jessica wasn't sure whether that was a good thing or bad. Only the coming days would tell.

NATHANIEL CONTINUED his cooperative ways by sleeping in the next morning. After awakening, Jessica lay in her bed for several moments before remembering the baby was in the house. Realizing he hadn't awakened her once during the night, she jumped from her bed, fearing something was wrong. But when she peered into his bassinet, she found him snoozing away as peaceful as a lamb.

Jessica went off to put some coffee on, then have her shower and get dressed. Nathaniel was stirring about the time she finished doing her hair. He needed a change. She put him in a clean diaper, deciding to give him a bath right before they left for Kate's place.

The morning went quickly. Jessica thought about Wiley's news as little as possible. There wasn't a thing she could do about the future, except to accept whatever fate brought her with as much grace as she could muster.

Kate had invited her to come in time for lunch—the other guests would be joining them for cake and coffee. Jessica left early because directions to the MacInnes place were complicated and she didn't want to get lost. As it turned out, she did miss a turn, but she eventually found the road to their ranch, arriving right on time.

As she got out of the car, she noticed Wiley's truck parked down by the barn, or a truck that looked just like his. She didn't see anybody around and wondered if maybe he'd come over to see John.

After retrieving Nathaniel from his car seat, Jessica carried him to the house. Kate, looking even more pregnant than the last time Jessica had seen her, opened the door before they got there.

"Howdy and welcome," Kate said, beaming.

Jessica felt buoyed by the woman's cheerfulness. "Hi." She slung her bag of supplies off her shoulder. Kate took it.

"Have anything else?"

"I brought Nathaniel's baby chair. It's in the car."

"Here, let me hold the little fella, if you want to get it."

Jessica handed the baby to Kate, then looked down in the direction of the barn. "Is Wiley here?"

"Yeah, he and John are talking horses. We got a new stallion and Wiley came to see it and talk to John about breeding it with one of his mares. At least, that's what he claimed. Frankly, I think he was just looking for an excuse to come over and see you."

Jessica smiled. "Why do you say that?"

"Because he asked when you'd be arriving. I told him for lunch and asked him if he wanted to join us, but he said he couldn't. He did want to say hello to you, though."

"Guess he'll see my car."

Kate nodded in the direction of the barn. "Looks like him coming now."

Two men came out of the barn and ambled toward Wiley's truck. "Well, I'll go get the seat," Jessica said, and headed back to the car. As she was pulling the baby chair out of the trunk, she heard a vehicle approach and the toot of a horn. Wiley pulled up next to her and stopped.

"All ready for the party, I see."

Jessica had put on a pair of white duck pants and a navy-and-white striped T-shirt. The look was clean, crisp and summery. Wiley had never seen her dressed quite this informally. "Kate said it was going to be casual. It's just a baby shower."

"You look real pretty."

"Thanks," she said, moving over to the open window on the passenger side.

"I know it's a ladies-only affair, but I brought you a present anyway." He picked up a wrapped present from the seat beside him and passed it over to her. It was a medium-size box with a big red ribbon on it. The bow was decidedly lopsided.

"How pretty. Did you wrap it?"

"Juana and I did it together. Between her tremor and my clumsiness, we had quite a time."

"It was very thoughtful."

"There's a little something for you in there, too, so you might want to open it later."

"Oh. Well, maybe I'll leave the gift here in the trunk and take it home with me."

Wiley nodded toward the house. "I'm keeping you from your lunch," he said.

"I'll see you tonight, though."

"You bet." Wiley gave her a wink. "Well, enjoy your baby shower."

He drove off. Jessica stood watching until the truck disappeared from sight. Confused feelings were welling up inside her. She hated not knowing what was going to happen.

BAR NONE, the shower was the most fun Jessica'd had in...well, years—at least with a group of other women. Aside from Jessica and Kate, about a dozen other women had been invited. Jessica knew Jamie Cole, and she'd met Wanda at the Cowboy Club. But she hadn't been introduced to Julia Sommers or her granddaughter-in-law, Erica McCormick.

Julia was the grandam of Red Rock society. She'd come to Colorado from Hollywood in the 1950s to make a film with Errol Flynn. Then, when she fell in love with a wealthy local rancher, she'd made Red Rock her home.

As thrilled as Jessica was to meet the woman, she was even happier to see Chloe again. They had a few minutes together to compare notes about babies and being newcomers to Red Rock before Jessica was introduced to some of the women who had been invited simply because they were concerned about Nathaniel. All of them had known Sally Anne and wanted to do what they could for her little boy.

As the women drank coffee and ate chocolate fudge cake, they talked about babies. When the discussion turned to romance, Jessica endured some gentle ribbing about just exactly what her relationship with Wiley might be.

"It's no wonder there's something kindling between the two of you," Julia said. "You had your first date at the Cowboy Club, didn't you?" Julia smiled when Jessica didn't hide her surprise. "I'm afraid things have a way of getting known in a small town. Crazy as it sounds, the Cowboy Club has a way of creating romance almost like magic. When I first came to town, we would film out at the old cowboy movie set during the day. At night, everyone in the cast would go to the club to rub shoulders with the real McCoy."

"And look where that got you," Wanda interjected.

Julia winked at her, then, turning to Jessica, she said, "One night, Hap McCormick came in. I was standing at the bar next to Errol Flynn—as gorgeous a man who ever walked on this earth, by the way—and when I turned, there was Hap, the genuine article. A tall and taciturn cowboy bigger than life and ten times more wonderful than any movie star." She fanned herself. "What can I say? I was hooked right then and there. Hap proposed to me at the Cowboy Club, and on our tenth wedding anniversary he bought me a half interest in it. I sold it to Dax a few years ago, but the club will always be special. It was our place."

As she finished, Julia wiped a tear from her eye and smiled.

"It's a pretty special place for me, too," Chloe said. "I felt a kind of magic the first time I went there, as if fate had led me to the Cowboy Club and Dax. That's where we met, too. I literally fell into his arms, right on the dance floor."

Everyone else chimed in and told their stories. Kate had met John when she started kindergarten, though they didn't date until high school. She told everyone that their first serious, going-out-to-dinner-together date had been at the Cowboy Club. And they'd been dancing at the club the night John proposed.

Erica admitted that her first date with Clay had been there, too, and he'd proposed to her in the same booth where his grandfather had asked Julia to marry him!

"Good heavens," Jessica said. "The place really is special. Not only did Wiley and I have our first date there, it's where I first laid eyes on Nathaniel."

The baby, who'd been sleeping quietly in his car seat, woke up on cue and squawked. Everyone laughed.

"I can tell right now that one will be a heartbreaker," Julia said.

"Amen," Jamie Cole added. She was sitting next to the baby and she reached over and stroked his cheek. "Would that I could meet a cowboy half as charming as this one."

"Your time will come," Wanda said. "It'll take someone real special for you, but he's out there somewhere."

"Yes," Kate agreed. "It only takes one. The right one, of course."

Jessica took a sip of coffee, wondering if she'd met the right one, or if she ever would. For a while, she had been sure that Wiley was the cowboy of her dreams. But since Nathaniel had become an issue between them, she was no longer certain. Maybe the love she was supposed to find at the Cowboy Club was the little cowboy, not the big one.

As soon as everyone finished their cake, Kate announced that it was time to tear into the loot. She had piled presents on the coffee table in the living room. Jessica was astonished at how terribly generous everyone was, but then, people in small towns did tend to open their hearts more readily.

There were lots of toys and clothes for the baby. Jamie had brought a bear dressed like a cowboy, and a children's Bible for him to use when he was older. Julia and

Erica had gone in together to purchase a brand-new crib. Wanda had gotten an adorable lamp of a cow jumping over the moon. Kate had knit a darling blue sweater and matching cap before she found out that her next was going to be a girl. The set was her gift to the baby. But Chloe's present was the hit of the party. She'd made a pair of baby-size cowboy boots for Nathaniel. They were fabricated from the softest kid available and they were absolutely adorable.

Jessica put them on the baby so that everyone could see. He kicked his legs and laughed. Kate took Polaroid photos of him and passed them around.

"There's no doubt this little buckeroo is going to break some poor girl's heart by the time he's in school. Maybe your girl's, Chloe."

She turned pink and looked down at her still-flat tummy. "Good heavens, you're right. Lord help us if we have a little girl. Dax will go around with a shotgun trying to protect her from the likes of charmers like Nathaniel."

"Well," Jamie said dryly, "thank goodness no one was around to protect you from Dax, or you wouldn't be here now!"

They all laughed over that, allowing that it was true. Not long afterward, the party broke up. Jessica was the last to leave. After thanking Kate for her hospitality, she left the baby in the house while she loaded the presents into the car. John MacInnes had promised to come by later that afternoon with the crib, which had to be transported in a truck.

When Jessica couldn't get another thing in the back seat of the car and still have room for the baby, she opened the trunk to put in the darling lamp Wanda had brought. As she did, Jessica saw the box with the big floppy red bow—Wiley's present. He had said there was something inside for her, too. Jessica wondered what it would be, and even more important, if it might give her a clue as to how their evening might go.

# 16

THE ROOM Sally Anne found was only half a mile from Union Station where she'd slept the first two nights. Now that she'd found a place to live, she felt better, but she knew she'd have to find a job soon or she'd be out on the street again.

That morning, she'd taken a bus along East Washington Street to a restaurant in Eastlake Park where she'd applied for a job washing dishes. The owner said he'd never had a girl want that job before. Mostly it was young guys with a car to support. The language in the kitchen could be coarse, he'd said. He'd have to give it some thought.

Sally Anne thought that was unfair and that there must be a law against it, but she was in no position to complain. In fact, she was lucky she hadn't been arrested. Monty had told her she'd better stay off the streets. By the time they'd gotten to Phoenix, the truck driver had pretty well figured out she was running away and that somebody would be looking for her. "If you run into trouble, leave me out of it," he'd said. "As far as I'm concerned, I don't know a thing."

Sally Anne had promised she would. They didn't talk about her baby, maybe because Monty knew it was better not to ask. And as far as she was concerned, just thinking about Nathaniel was more than she could handle.

Alone in her room in Phoenix, five hundred miles from anyplace she could call home, she found out how hard loneliness could be. Nathaniel had been a terrible burden, but he had been company. It surprised her how much she missed him—not the struggle, of course, but having someone to care about besides herself.

There hadn't been a soul around when she'd left the basket outside the Cowboy Club. She sure hoped Nathaniel hadn't had to wait long before somebody found him and called Wiley Cooper. She worried that things hadn't gone according to plan. A fear was starting to gnaw at her. She wanted to know he was all right.

More than once, she'd considered calling the Double C Ranch, just to make sure Nathaniel was there. If she knew her baby was okay, she thought it would be easier to put him from her mind and get on with her own life. Besides, Mr. Cooper might have some questions.

Deciding she needed to clear her head before she phoned, Sally Anne left the tiny room she rented to walk around the neighborhood. The fear that Mr. Cooper might be able to trace her call worried her until she decided to use a pay phone. There was one at the service station not far from where she lived. It should be safe enough.

Having made her decision, she went to the phone and placed a collect call, using the number on a slip of paper in her wallet. Hearing the phone ringing at the other end, she got nervous.

Wiley answered on the second ring. "Sally Anne?" he said after telling the operator he'd accept the charges. "Where are you?"

She ignored the question. "Did you find Nathaniel all right?" she asked, nearly breaking into tears.

"Yes, sweetheart, we did. But everybody's worried about you."

"My baby's okay?"

"He's fine. A very nice lady in town is taking care of him until you get back."

"I wanted you to take care of him, not somebody I

don't even know," she lamented. "Anyway, I'm not going back to Colorado."

"Listen to me, Sally Anne, you're too young to be on your own. You belong here in Red Rock, with your baby."

"No. He's better off with you. I love him, but I can't take care of him. Didn't you read my note?"

"Yes, sweetheart, I did. But you aren't thinking clearly. You need to come home and we need to talk about this. If you need money, I'll help you. Your dad would expect that and that's what I'll do."

Sally Anne began to cry. "I can't take care of Nathaniel as good as you. Please, Mr. Cooper, just take care of my baby so I won't worry. Please."

"Tell me where you are, Sally Anne, and I'll come get you."

All she could do was sob. This was much worse than she thought it would be. Much harder.

"If we sit down together and talk this thing out," Wiley said, "we can solve it."

Sally Anne continued to cry. Why couldn't Wiley Cooper understand that her baby was better off with him than with her? Why didn't he want to help her? He had been real close to her dad, and she'd been so sure he would help.

But she knew that she couldn't argue. If he didn't understand, then he didn't. So, deciding it was no use to talk, she softly said goodbye and hung up, wiping her eyes with the back of her hand before slowly walking back to the boardinghouse.

WILEY WALKED from his truck to Jessica's front door, knowing this was going to be one of the more difficult evenings of his life. He had a bottle of French champagne in his hand, but he was hardly in a mood to celebrate. Jessica was bound to be disappointed by his news, and probably angry when she heard what he'd done after his conversation with Sally Anne. But there was no running from it. He had to tell her; he had to face the issue.

Jessica opened the door. Holding it open with one hand, she balanced Nathaniel on her shoulder. She was rubbing the baby's back, smiling at him and looking pretty as could be in a soft yellow sleeveless sundress with a short skirt and white sandals.

"Evening, Wiley," she said, oblivious to what was coming.

The sight of her smiling face made his heart ache. Worse, she looked natural and completely at ease with the baby in her arms. He could tell she'd come a long way since she'd first laid eyes on Nathaniel.

"How'd the party go?" he asked, entering.

"See for yourself," she said, pointing to the plethora of gifts arrayed on the sideboard. "Everybody was so generous. The care and the love was incredible. This town has really opened its heart to this little cowboy." She closed the door and resumed rubbing the baby's back. "Nathaniel's going to bed soon, but he wanted to stay up and thank you for his present."

"Oh, it wasn't anything," Wiley said, lowering his eyes.

"It was the only baseball glove he got," she said, chuckling. "You're definitely an original thinker."

He smiled self-consciously. "It was kind of silly considering he won't be able to use it for years, but I didn't know what else to get."

"It was very sweet, and much appreciated, believe me." She turned so that Nathaniel's face was toward Wiley. "Tell him, sweetie pie. Can you say thanks?" Jessica laughed and gave the baby's bottom a gentle pat. "Darn, the little rascal was saying his lines perfectly all afternoon."

Wiley smiled as best he could. Her upbeat mood, delightful as it was, only made this harder for him. He really hated himself just then.

"I'm guessing the champagne flutes you got me are for immediate use," she went on, "if that bottle in your hand is what I think it is."

"Yep, it's for you."

"Not us?"

He kind of shrugged, his insides twisting. "Sure. But I do want to talk to you a bit, Jessica."

She gave him a questioning look, finally picking up on his somber mood. "Why don't I put Nathaniel down, then? You can open the champagne, unless you think it wouldn't fit the occasion."

"I'll leave that up to you."

"Oh, my," she said, her cheerfulness in full retreat. "Well, give me a minute."

Wiley sat on the sofa, knowing that it all went back to that awful day when he'd told Lucas he wanted that bronco broken. If he'd listened instead of giving orders, Lucas wouldn't have died, Sally Anne might never have had a baby, and he and Jessica would not be where they were right now. So many lives had been changed, and often for the worse.

Jessica returned in a couple of minutes. She sat on the edge of the green leather chair as if she knew she wasn't going to like what he had to say. "What's happened, Wiley?"

"I got a call from Sally Anne this afternoon."

She calculated the words. "And?"

"She called me collect, so afterward, I phoned the sheriff to see if they could trace the call. They did and the police in Phoenix have already been alerted. I'm flying down there with Quentin Starr in his plane first thing in the morning. Chances are, she'll be found."

"And you'll be bringing her back."

Wiley nodded. "That's the plan."

"You're warning me that Nathaniel's days with me are numbered."

He felt a terrible pain inside. "One way or the other, that's most likely the case."

Jessica stared off for a moment or two, looking as though she was gathering her courage. "It's not like you didn't warn me."

"She's just a mixed-up kid in need of guidance," Wiley said.

"Did she say she wants her baby back?"

"No, but once she gets her life straightened out, I'd say it's likely she will."

Jessica wrung her hands nervously. "That's what you're hoping, isn't it?"

"I'm hoping for what's best for all concerned."

"What's best for Nathaniel and Sally Anne, in other words."

"I'd like to think you, too, Jessica."

Her smile was brittle. "That's one decision I'm capable of making for myself."

Wiley lowered his eyes. This was probably inevitable, but he hated it anyway. "You may not give a lick, Jessica, but this is one of the hardest things I've ever had to do."

"Oh, I know you're not enjoying it."

"If Sally Anne was your daughter, wouldn't you want her home, with her baby?"

"That's not an easy question to answer, Wiley. It depends on a lot of things. It may or may not be best for a child to be with his natural parents."

"Is that an objective statement?"

"No less objective than you deciding Nathaniel ought to be with Sally Anne."

"I don't know that I decided that," he said, maybe a little too quickly.

"I do. I think you see it as being in *your* best interest."

Her words hurt but he couldn't blame her. "I'd like to think I'm not that selfish."

"Oh, I'm sure you *believe* what you want is best for everybody. You don't have a cruel bone in your body, Wiley. I'll give you that. But you've got blinders on."

He gave her a long, hard look. "And you don't?"

"We see the situation differently. Maybe we should leave it at that. I've got a nice dinner planned. There's no reason we can't be friendly and share a pleasant meal." She returned his hard gaze. "I'm not pleased about this, but I don't blame you."

He almost wished she would. It would be easier. As it was, he felt like an insensitive brute, though it wasn't as if he wanted anything that the law wouldn't probably require in the long run anyway. Sally Anne had a good chance of ending up with her baby in the end. All she needed was help, and he was prepared to give it to her, not for selfish reasons, but because he felt obligated. The easiest thing in the world would be to walk away.

"Now, if you'll excuse me," Jessica said, getting up, "I've got some work to do in the kitchen."

Wiley watched her go, feeling as though his hopes, his dreams, perhaps even his happiness, were walking out with her. He was trapped between love and duty and there was no easy way out, perhaps no way out at all.

WHEN JESSICA TOLD Wiley good-night, she knew it would be the last time she'd see him...at least under romantic circumstances. He must have sensed it was the end, as well, because he didn't even try to kiss her. The way she figured it, the day might come when they could be friends again, but nothing more.

"I'm terribly, terribly sorry," he said, touching her arm.

Jessica nodded, but she couldn't keep the tears from coming. She closed the door as quickly as she could and

ran to get Nathaniel, clutching him to her breast, aware
for the first time that as much harm as good had been
caused by her love. This little boy had opened her heart
and filled it with love again, but when he left it would be
empty once more. One step forward and two steps back.

Sunday morning, Jessica went to hear Jamie Cole's ser-
mon on love without conditions. By the end of the service, Jessica had done enough soul-searching to realize
that she'd been more than a little selfish herself. She also
realized that maybe she didn't belong in Red Rock. The
people were wonderful here and she'd already made
friends, but perhaps she had learned the lesson God had
wanted her to and it was time to move on.

As she thought about that, she wondered if leaving
proved that her love was unconditional, or that it was basically selfish. Her decision would affect her uncle more
than anyone else, so she decided she owed it to him to
discuss the matter.

When she and Nathaniel dropped by Ford's house on
their way home from church, she found her uncle in his
bathrobe and pajamas reading the Sunday *Denver Post*.
"What an unexpected pleasure," he said. "A Sunday
visit from family. Can't remember the last time that's
happened."

He had some coffee on the stove and got them each a
cup. Jessica put Nathaniel on a blanket on the living-
room floor. He liked to crawl around some and Kate had
suggested that she give the "little cowboy" a chance to
test his range.

"So, what brings you by on a Sunday morning?" Ford
asked, the tone of his voice signaling that he felt something coming.

"You've heard the news about Sally Anne?"

"Yes," Ford replied. "I have."

"I probably made a big mistake taking her baby into
my home and heart," Jessica said, "but for better or

worse, I did it. Now I'm left with the question of what to do with myself."

"You're saying the situation calls for you to take some kind of action."

She nodded. "The easiest course would be to go home to Dallas, but that would have a very definite impact on you, Uncle Ford. I've probably been selfish enough. On the other hand, it might not be that big a deal to you. I guess what I'm asking is how you would feel if I packed up my tent and left."

Ford considered the question, fingering his coffee cup. Then he looked at her with watery blue eyes, his lips pressed tight together. "I wouldn't be thrilled, Jessica, obviously. We're only getting started in the practice, but I've been enjoying your being a part of it already. The more important question is where you'll be happy. You living in Red Rock can't be for my benefit. In the long run, it'll never work."

"Do you think I'd be a coward to leave?"

"Coward's not the word I'd choose. The question I'd ask is, what are you running from or to?"

Jessica thought for a while. "I guess I feel confused about whether I dare love again or not. I might have been lonely in Dallas, but at least things were on an even keel."

"You're saying predictability is important?"

"I'm saying I don't want to keep losing the things I love," she replied, tears spurting from her eyes.

"We're talking about Nathaniel."

"We're talking about Wiley, too. I allowed myself to love both of them. Wiley's let me down."

"On purpose?"

"No, of course not. He may even feel as betrayed as I do. We're just of two different minds, Uncle Ford, and no amount of talk and mediation can change that. Sometimes you simply have to face up to the fact that what is, is."

"So, you're saying you *want* to go back to Dallas."

"I don't *want* to. But it's starting to look like the logical thing to do. I know the place, I know people there and I can probably find work."

"If that's what you want, Jessica, I won't stand in your way. You're free to do what's in your heart, no questions asked."

She could see that her uncle was doing the loving thing and without conditions. "Thank you," she said, wiping her eyes. "That means the world to me."

Jessica went home and gave the matter a whole lot of thought. She realized that she'd become a complication. Red Rock's first obligation was to Nathaniel and Sally Anne. Wiley's feelings about what was right were clear. Jessica knew she'd be in the way, and maybe the simplest and cleanest thing was to eliminate the problem. Others could provide short-term care for Nathaniel. Yes, it seemed obvious to her—the best thing to do was to get out of the way, the sooner the better.

Feeling relief at having made her decision, Jessica called her uncle first. Ford told her he'd hoped otherwise, but was determined to support her decision, no matter what.

"I'm going to call Ivy Dix first thing in the morning," she told him. "If Sally Anne decides she wants her baby back, and the court agrees to let her have him, going fifty miles to pick him up in Cortez won't be the end of the world."

"Once you make up your mind, you have a way of moving fast, don't you, honey?"

"Let's just say I woke up, realizing that I've been selfish. This whole business with Nathaniel has been for my benefit and me leaving will be best for everyone."

"You don't think you might be overreacting a mite?"

"No, Uncle Ford. I've become part of the problem, not the solution."

It was a hard decision for her, but Jessica went to bed that night knowing she was doing the right thing.

WILEY AND QUENTIN STARR spent two days on the problem, conferring with officials in both Arizona and Colorado. They finally got permission to take Sally Anne back to Red Rock, provided the girl agreed not to contest extradition. Wiley went to the Maricopa County Juvenile Detention Center to see her. She'd been there since her arrest Sunday morning.

The place had an institutional feel, but fell short of the atmosphere of a prison. Wiley met with her in a visiting room furnished with a sofa and upholstered chairs. Sally Anne was sullen as she sat down, refusing to look at him.

"I thought you'd help me," she lamented as she stared down at her hands folded in her lap, "not turn me in to the police."

"Sally Anne, you're much too young to be out on your own."

"I'd have been just fine if it wasn't for you."

"What did you think you were going to do? What were your plans?"

"I was going to get a job. Then I was going to get my high school diploma. Then I was going to nursing school."

"That's a laudable goal, but wouldn't you like a little help?"

"You mean like the way you helped me by calling the cops?"

"No, that's not what I mean. You still have choices. I've got things worked out so that you'll be released to my custody once we get back to Red Rock. You'll have to deal with the consequences of what you did, but with my help, and the help of the community, you should be able to return to a normal life with your baby."

"Didn't you listen to what I said?" Sally Anne said. "Didn't you read my note? I want Nathaniel to grow up in Red Rock, with parents who love him and can take care of him. I can't do that. And I need to know he's okay before I can start over."

"You'll get help. I know you can't handle everything on your own and still take care of Nathaniel."

She looked up at him then. "What if I don't want him?"

Wiley regarded her blankly.

"That doesn't make me bad," Sally Anne went on. "Don't you think it was hard for me to give him up? You think I liked leaving him? I hated it, but I know it's better for him and it's better for me. And now you've messed everything up!"

"Things are not messed up. Besides, Nathaniel's your child."

"Oh, yeah? Well, why did you let that other man adopt *your* daughter? How come you didn't keep her and raise her yourself?"

Wiley blinked. "How did you know about that?" he asked.

"My dad told me. He said how you let your daughter go because she was young and you had lots you wanted to do with your life."

"That was different. My daughter went to live with her mother."

"Yeah, but you never wanted to see her. She was out of your life."

"I *wanted* to see her," Wiley said defensively, "but it was better that I didn't."

"Better for who?"

He shifted uneasily. "Better for everybody."

"Yeah, well, I think that other man did you a big favor.

You were young and he was old. He wanted a daughter and you didn't. How come you won't do that for me? That man gave you a chance to do what you needed to do with your life. I want that chance, too. I want to be a nurse."

"What about your baby?"

"What about yours?"

Wiley could see she had her mind set. He could also see he'd made assumptions that weren't valid. "This is something we can discuss with the judge and the county social worker. You may be entitled to live your life, but you also need to accept your responsibilities. We all do. One of the reasons I'm here is that I feel responsible for you."

"Then why not help me become a nurse?"

"That's something we can discuss."

"And what about Nathaniel?" she asked.

"What do you want for your baby, Sally Anne?"

"I told you," she said, her eyes tearing up. "I want him to be happy."

Wiley sat there, the lump in his throat growing. He'd seen tears from two women over this baby. The irony was, they weren't fighting over who got Nathaniel now. To the contrary, they each wanted pretty much the same thing. *He* was the one standing in the way. *He* was the one who'd been blind and pigheaded, certain he knew what was best for everyone else.

"Tell you what," Wiley said. "Let's go back to Red Rock and we'll all talk about this. If what you really want is to put your baby up for adoption and to go on and finish your schooling, I'll do my best to see that happens."

"Do *you* want Nathaniel?" the girl asked, wiping her eyes. "Would you raise him on the Double C?"

"That's something I'll have to think about long and hard. But I can tell you this, Sally Anne, I know a lady who'd probably just love to be Nathaniel's mom."

"A friend of yours?"

"A very good friend," Wiley said with a smile.

Sally Anne smiled, too. "Is she your girlfriend?"

"God only knows. But that's another reason we have to get back to Colorado. Will you come back with me, Sally Anne?"

She looked at him, then down at her hands. "Are you going to make me see my baby?"

Wiley shook his head. "Not if you don't want to."

"I'm not saying I never want to see him again," Sally Anne said, wiping away another tear as she faced him once more, "but not until he's old enough to decide he wants to see me, too."

Wiley realized how wise the child was, how much wiser she was than he. "I understand that," he said, thinking of Lindsay. "I truly do."

And he did.

# 17

IT WAS LATE Tuesday night by the time Wiley, Sally Anne and Quentin Starr arrived back in Red Rock. Wiley had tried phoning Jessica, but hadn't gotten an answer. But he'd alerted Juana to have a room prepared for Sally Anne.

When they reached the Double C, Sally Anne was asleep, her head propped against the passenger-side window of the truck. They had to be in Cortez to meet with the county authorities early the next morning, so Wiley figured the first order of business was to let the poor girl get some rest.

Juana was waiting at the door as he led the sleepy teenager to the house. Sally Anne didn't have a whole lot in the way of luggage, but Wiley carried what she had in from the truck. Seeing the housekeeper had everything well in hand, he told her he was going into town, and he took off.

It was midnight by the time he reached Jessica's place. The little house was dark, but Wiley decided to risk her ire by waking her and the baby anyway. Several minutes of knocking and ringing the bell didn't rouse a soul and he realized that no one was at home. Where could she be? A neighbor, having heard all the racket, came out of his house.

Seeing it was Wiley, he said, "Miss Kilmer left early this morning, headed back to Texas."

"What?"

"That's what she told the wife."

"With the baby?"

"No, that Dix woman from the county came and got him yesterday."

Wiley was so stunned it was all he could do to thank the man and leave. His first thought was to head for Ford's house to confirm the information, but when he got in his truck he just sat there, feeling as if someone had pulled out his guts and stomped on them. It was several minutes before he was able to get enough control of himself to drive.

Ford did not look pleased at being roused from a sound sleep, but Wiley had to know what in the hell was going on.

"An old codger needs his rest," Ford lamented. "Especially when he's back to doing the work of two."

"Why did she leave?"

"She wrote you a letter, Wiley. No sense in me trying to explain when you can read it for yourself. Come on in," he said, going to the table next to his big easy chair. Picking up an envelope, he handed it to Wiley. "You want to look at it here, or take it home with you?"

"I'll read it now, if you don't mind."

"Then I'll get myself a glass of warm milk. Want some?"

"No, thanks." Wiley dropped onto the sofa and tore open the envelope. His hands shaking, he read:

Dear Wiley,

Don't hate me for leaving without saying good-bye. It seemed best for everyone's sake. My feelings for you are much deeper than my actions would indicate. But I also know that regard for someone, even love, are only a part of the picture. The things that separate two people may be even more important than the things that connect them.

Knowing both you and Nathaniel has changed

my life, but because our needs and our desires are so different, in the long run, we would only torture each other. Resentment would surely follow, then unhappiness. It is in both our interests, as well as Sally Anne's and Nathaniel's, that I move on now, when a new beginning and a new direction are easier and less painful.

I cannot close without saying that you gave me so much, including lovely memories, and I shall always be grateful.

                                                    Jessica

Wiley groaned, then read over the letter once again. He shook his head, falling back in the chair, dazed. How sad and ironic that this would happen, just when he was beginning to see things differently. Sally Anne had opened his eyes to the fact that he'd been guided by his fears and his past experiences as much as by reason. Not only that, he'd manufactured obligations he didn't have just so he wouldn't have to deal with those fears.

Ford returned to the front room with his glass of milk. He plopped down on the sofa and gave Wiley a level look. "You see why I've been a bachelor all these years."

"I've been such a fool."

Ford sipped his milk. "You want to talk about it?"

"When we met, Jessica and I were both gun-shy about having kids in our lives, which made us perfect for each other. Then Nathaniel came along. She learned from the experience and changed the way she felt. I didn't."

"So, you have different goals."

"Yep, in a nutshell, that's it."

"What are you going to do now?"

"I've got a lot of thinking to do, not to mention a lot of problems, legal and otherwise, that need sorting out."

"I can educate you on the law," Ford said, "but not on women and children."

"Well, I've got to start someplace."

"Would you mind coming to see me in my office tomorrow? I'm a better lawyer at nine in the morning than I am at 1:00 a.m."

"Okay, fine, but let me ask you one thing. Do you think Jessica loves me?"

"How in tarnation would I know?"

"I thought she might have said something."

"It was clear to me she likes you, Wiley, but beyond that, you'd know better than I. Contracts and torts are my thing, not the ways of a woman's heart."

Wiley got up. "I can see I've got a lot of work ahead of me. I'll be by your office first thing in the morning."

"I'll be waitin'."

Wiley left then, knowing pretty much what he wanted. The trick would be getting from here to there. The worst part was, a hell of a lot seemed to be standing in his way.

THE SECOND NIGHT Jessica was in Dallas she decided that attempting to pick up her life where she'd left off would probably be a mistake. Eventually she'd have to get a job, but before she started looking, she needed to clear her mind of Red Rock, Wiley Cooper and Nathaniel Springer. She needed to take a trip, go someplace completely different, get her mind off her disappointments. She needed a break from reality.

Jessica had had a friend in law school, a woman from San Antonio named Sue Ellen Williams, who'd gone off to New York to practice law and make her fortune. A couple of times before Jessica married Geoff, Sue Ellen had suggested she come to the Big Apple and sample the high life. Jessica had made one trip to see her friend. They'd had fun, but it had been enough to convince Jessica that the bright lights of Manhattan were not for her. Shortly after that trip, she'd met Geoff, married, and Sue

Ellen became just another name on Jessica's Christmas-card list.

Maybe it was a sign of the degree of her desperation, but Jessica fastened on the notion of getting hold of Sue Ellen again and seeing if she could wrangle another invitation to the big city. It wasn't until her fourth day back in Dallas that she finally worked up the courage to make the call.

"You can't imagine what a lovely surprise it is to hear your voice," Sue Ellen said. "I've thought of you often since hearing about your terrible loss."

Sue Ellen had written Jessica a very nice note after Geoff and Cassandra had died, but like everything else, responding to it had been lost in the terrible blur of those painful weeks and months.

"I remember saying to myself," Sue Ellen went on, "that I ought to invite you to come and see me when the time was right, and I can't tell you how ashamed I am that I never did."

Jessica gave her friend a thumbnail account of the recent developments in her life.

"This is the perfect time for you to come to New York, then," Sue Ellen said. "I'm warning you, sugar, I won't take no for an answer this time. They made me an associate partner at the firm this past year. I've got myself a brand-new apartment on the Upper East Side with a lovely guest room and a friend who can get tickets to any show in town. Please come!"

Jessica was just needy enough to take her up on it. Sue Ellen didn't lack for courage—she'd tell Jessica if and when she'd worn out her welcome. Jessica figured five days to a week would do the trick. So she made plane reservations and called her Uncle Ford, to let him know she'd be out of town for a while. He'd promised to have the things shipped she hadn't been able to get into the car. The plan was for him to hold off with her stuff until she returned.

"New York ought to be a change of pace for you after Red Rock," he said.

"It won't inconvenience you?"

"Not a bit. Cody's house was sitting empty before you got here, I reckon it'll sit empty again unless Dax's in-laws want it. They're coming from New York to live closer to Chloe. If they show up soon, I can always store your stuff over here."

"I'm glad my leaving is convenient for someone," she said with a sigh. "So, how are you?"

"Busy as a one-armed paper hanger."

"You don't hate me?"

"Of course not. Figured out long ago there's no percentage in blaming your problems on others. Besides, you were within your rights."

"I don't imagine everybody else is quite as generous."

"By 'everybody else,' you're meaning Wiley Cooper, I take it."

"For example."

"Wiley's pretty busy himself, what with trying to sort out the lives of a couple of kids, not to mention his own."

"I'm sure he feels I left him holding the bag."

"Wiley's no more one to cast blame than I am. Anyway, Sally Anne and her baby were not your problem. He knows that and so does everyone else."

Her uncle was being charitable. There wasn't anything to admire in a person who took off, leaving others to sort out a problem. Even so, Jessica was convinced that what she'd done was in everybody's best interests, long term. She just wished she knew Wiley had accepted that—*really* accepted it.

"I'll be in touch when I get back to Dallas," she said. "I'm leaving next Monday and should be getting back the following Sunday."

"Who is it you're visiting?"

"Sue Ellen Williams, an old friend from law school."

"Oh. Don't believe I heard you mention the name. Well, you have fun, honey."

"Yeah," Jessica said sadly. "I'll try."

THE FOUR OF THEM came out of the theater with the rest of the crowd. Sue Ellen and her current squeeze, Jordan Matheson, a corporate lawyer, said their goodbyes and headed off to his place. It was the third time this week, making Jessica feel like an interloper. "Oh, don't be silly," Sue Ellen assured her. "His mattress is better than mine. Plus, this way you get some privacy, too."

Once the other couple was gone, Richard Valenti, the tax attorney Sue Ellen had fixed Jessica up with, gave her that gee-here-we-are, just-the-two-of-us look. "Buy you a drink?"

"I'd love to, Richard, but I'm bushed. I think I'll just go home."

"We're both headed for the Upper East Side. Might as well share a cab."

Jessica didn't object. All the way uptown in the taxi she listened to him talk, not so subtly putting a move on her. Richard apparently figured his friend was scoring, so to maintain his pride, he ought to be scoring, too.

It was the second time Jessica had been fixed up since arriving. The only reason she'd agreed was not to offend Sue Ellen. Fortunately, tomorrow was Sunday and she'd be leaving for home.

Actually, the trip as a whole hadn't been as unpleasant as the dates she'd been on. Sue Ellen had been generous to a fault. Jessica had spent most of her days walking around town, visiting museums and galleries or taking in a matinee. The change of scene had been good for her—she'd gotten in a lot of thinking. She realized that the bright lights of New York made for an interesting change of pace, but the slow easy rhythms of Red Rock and the simple honesty of the people there were much more in keeping with her own nature. Even Dallas seemed too large and impersonal. And yes, she missed Wiley and Nathaniel. It took New York to show her just how empty she felt without them.

Richard, meanwhile, was hitting on her again. She plucked his hand off her knee. As they came to Sue Ellen's building, he began lobbying to come inside. Jessica looked him right in the eye. "Richard, thank you, but no!" Then she pressed a ten-dollar bill in his hand to cover her share of the cab fare and jumped out, not waiting for a reply.

It was a warm, balmy evening and Jessica would have loved to go for a stroll, and she probably could have safely, provided she kept her eyes straight ahead and walked at a quick, determined pace. But she didn't need the hassle. Instead, she'd go inside and read a book. Sighing, she went to the building entrance, pulled open the door and stepped into the small lobby containing a sofa, a few chairs and potted palms. What she saw made her mouth drop open.

Standing next to the sofa was the building superintendent, looking down at a man in a cowboy hat changing the diaper of a fussy baby. When the man turned his head in her direction, she saw it was Wiley.

"Oh, there she is!" he said. "Perfect timing, Jessica. If you'd arrived five minutes earlier, you could have cleaned up the mess."

She was too shocked to speak. Instead, she moved over to the sofa. The super, thoroughly amused, nodded a greeting. The baby, who continued to fuss, was Nathaniel, of course. Wiley secured the last tape on the disposable diaper, pulled down the little boy's shirt, picked him up and stood.

Jessica shook her head with disbelief. "What on earth are you doing here?"

Wiley wiped a drip of drool from the baby's chin with his knuckle. "We didn't come to give a speech at the U.N."

"Yes, that I believe."

He looked down at the dirty diaper on the floor, then at the super. "Sorry about that, partner. Would you mind disposing of it for me?"

"Can't think of anything I'd rather do, mack." But he said it with a smile. Bending over, he picked up the diaper, then went off.

Wiley turned Nathaniel to face Jessica, one hand under the baby's bottom to support him, the other around the baby's chest. "So, how's New York?"

She blinked. "Never mind New York, I'm still in shock. Explain what's going on, Wiley."

"Well, we missed you and, since Nathaniel's never been to Gotham, I thought I'd give him his first taste."

"Wiley," she said, putting her hands on her hips.

"Okay, here's the story. Sally Anne doesn't want to raise a child. She realizes that she needs to grow up and get educated before she takes on those kinds of responsibilities. She wants me to adopt Nathaniel. She thinks I need to raise a baby for myself, as well as for her, and she insists that I might learn something in the process. After giving it a lot of thought, I decided she might be right. My problem isn't children so much as it is guilt and fear."

Jessica looked at the baby she'd been trying so hard to put from her mind. "How did you get permission to bring Nathaniel here?"

"I didn't, exactly. I've petitioned the court for Sally Anne and me to have joint custody pending legal adoption. She's staying in the house she lived in with her dad, and Juana and I are looking after Nathaniel, with some help from Jamie and Ruthie and Kate and Chloe. Sally Anne still has criminal charges to face, but Ford has worked things out with the prosecutor. She'll get probation on condition that she finishes high school and goes on to nursing school. I'm arranging for her to attend a boarding school in Denver at my expense. We've agreed to an open adoption, which means she'll have access to Nathaniel when she wants, but I'll have custody. As far as coming to New York is concerned, basically, I got on a plane."

"Why?"

Wiley shifted uncomfortably. "That's a little more delicate to explain."

"I'm all ears."

He looked her dead in the eye. "I guess what it boils down to is that I love you, Jessica. I'd like for us to be a family—you, me and Nathaniel. You love him and he loves you and I was…well, hoping to fit in the mix."

Jessica bit her lip, her eyes welling. "You big, dumb cowboy," she said, the tears starting to run down her cheeks. "I'd never agree to be with you just because of Nathaniel. It would have to be because of you, because we belonged together."

Wiley looked down at the baby. "You aren't saying he's a problem for you, are you?"

"No, I'm saying everything has to start with you and me. I wouldn't want you just to get him. And I wouldn't want you taking him just to get me."

Wiley shook his head. "This is getting too complicated. Jessica, do you love me? Yes or no?"

"Yes," she said, wiping her eyes.

"Okay, that's good to hear because I love you, too. Now we've got to decide about him." Wiley's voice grew gentle. "Are you ready to be a mother again?"

Jessica couldn't help herself. She took Nathaniel from

him, sobbing as she did, kissing and hugging him. Wiley watched, grinning, his eyes filling.

"Now, how about me?"

She laughed, wiping her nose and eyes. Then she threw an arm around his neck and gave him a big, sensuous kiss. "You crazy cowpoke," she said. "I do love you."

Just then, two women came in the door. As they walked past, they grinned with amusement. "Will you look at that," one said. "A baby and a cowboy."

"Lucky girl," the other said as they went into the elevator.

Jessica and Wiley regarded each other, laughing.

"They'll never know how lucky," she said, kissing his lips and cheek. "Never."

# Epilogue

WILEY PUT another log on the fire in the private cottage they had rented in Vail. The plan was to spend the first week of their marriage there, then fly to San Francisco for the remainder of their honeymoon. Jessica had headed off to take a bubble bath about ten minutes earlier. The cottage was tiny enough that he could hear her splashing and singing. She sounded so happy it brought tears to his eyes. He had a lot to be thankful for, and he knew it.

He looked around the room. Everything was perfect. The fire was going nicely. A bottle of French champagne, courtesy of Dax and Chloe, was chilling in an ice bucket. Wiley had taken off his jacket and tie but was still dressed. Jessica had slipped out of her wedding shoes as soon as they were in the door. He looked at them now, lined up by the chocolate-brown leather couch that faced the love seat. The shoes seemed so lovely and delicate—just like Jessica herself. Chloe had designed and made them to match Jessica's dress.

As long as he lived, Wiley would never forget the vision of his bride that morning. He'd stood in front of the altar at the community church. Dax was his best man. When the wedding march had begun, and he'd turned and watched Ford escort Jessica down the aisle, it had been the proudest moment of his life.

He sighed. This had been a big week, to put it mildly. On Wednesday, they had a party to celebrate Nathaniel's first birthday. Ford had been there and so had Jamie, along with Erica and Clay and Chloe and Dax. Kate and

John MacInnes hadn't been able to make it because their daughter, Elisabeth Anne, had been born the day before.

Then, on Thursday, while Julia and Erica hosted a bridal shower for Jessica out at the Lone Eagle Ranch, the Thursday-night poker group had thrown a bachelor party for Wiley. Clay, who wasn't much of a card player, had joined them.

Wiley had wondered out loud if the guys were going to have some kind of exotic dancer jump out of a cake. Dax had chuckled. "Not likely, though I did think about asking Wanda if she wanted to give it a go."

Everyone had laughed at that, except Heath. "Gee, Dax, I don't know why you'd want to hire some stranger. Jamie Cole has the best legs in town."

Dax's eyebrows had shot up at that comment. "That's the second time you've said that, Heath. You got a crush on the minister?"

Heath had turned beet red. Clay had taken pity on poor Heath and had changed the subject, announcing that Clay's sister was coming back to Colorado.

"To stay this time, or just for a visit?" Quentin had asked a shade too quickly.

Wiley had heard the interest in Quentin's voice right along with everyone else. He hadn't forgotten that when Quentin was the town's certified bad boy back in high school, he'd had an awful crush on Clay's little sister. Of course, Kiley hadn't given Quentin the time of day then, but who knew what might happen now? Love was definitely in the air.

Ford must have felt that way, too. "Hell's bells," the old pettifogger said, "if this keeps up, I'll be the only bachelor left in Red Rock. Of course, that might not be all bad—"

Wiley had promised that if that ever happened, he'd put a big photo of Ford on the front page of the *Recorder*, saying that the town's only bachelor was up for grabs and all ladies between eighteen and eighty could apply.

The mayor had shivered. "Does that include Myra Bridges?"

Wiley had nodded solemnly.

"Then I think I'll pass. But thank you kindly for the thought anyway, Wiley."

Their game had broken up after that and Wiley had had a good laugh when he told Jessica about it. She'd had fun at her shower, too. The women had gone in together to get her an outfit for their wedding night. Some kind of filmy gown-and-robe set, she said, though she'd refused to let him see it. Jessica insisted she wanted to surprise him.

Wiley heard the sound of the hair dryer and checked his watch again. He wouldn't have long to wait now. In a few minutes, his bride would step out of the bathroom and their life together would begin. They would have a wonderful marriage, he was sure of it. He'd listened closely to the words Jamie had said that morning. And he knew he would love Jessica and cherish her always.

After a while, the sound of the dryer stopped. Wiley stood in front of the fireplace, facing the bedroom, as he waited.

The door opened then and Jessica came toward him. She was wearing a lacy turquoise robe that brought out the color of her eyes. Her slippers matched the robe, and if Wiley had to bet, he'd guess that Chloe had made them.

He held out his arms. "If you aren't the most beautiful thing I've ever seen in my life, I don't know what is," he said.

Jessica slipped into his embrace, locked her arms around his neck and kissed him long and hard. Then her lips softened, parted and she moaned, leaning into him so that their bodies were pressed together. When she finally pulled back, she said, "I've been thinking about that ever since I got in the tub."

He kissed her nose. "Then why did it take you twenty-four minutes to get out here?"

She laughed. "You timed me?"

"You bet."

Jessica kissed his cheek. "Anxious to get this marriage consummated, Mr. Cooper?"

He poked his tongue in his cheek. "No, but if this champagne gets much colder, it might freeze."

"Well, we can't let that happen, can we? Why don't you open it?"

He went over to the bottle, pulled it from the ice bucket, opened it and poured some into two glasses. Jessica watched him from her place in front of the fire. With the light behind her, he could see her body clearly. It looked as if she didn't have a stitch on under that lacy robe.

He handed her a glass. "To the woman I love."

She blushed. "And to the cowboy I love."

They each took a long sip of wine. Then Wiley took her glass and set it down on the mantel, next to his, and took her in his arms. "What do you have on under that robe, Mrs. Cooper?"

"Nothing."

"That's what I thought." He reached over and undid the tie at her waist, letting the robe fall open. "Didn't they give you a matching gown?"

She nodded. "But I'm saving it."

He blinked. "What for?"

Jessica gave his chin a kiss, "Our golden wedding anniversary. I figured you wouldn't want to waste the time taking it off tonight. But in another fifty years you might not be in such a hurry to get me out of it."

Wiley scooped her into his arms and strode toward the bedroom. "You know, Jessica, that's the only dumb thing

I've ever heard you say. What makes you think I'm going to slow down by then? Hell, I'll only be ninety. And you'll be a sexy eighty-two."

She giggled as he settled her on the bed. "Well, if that's the case, I guess I'll save it for our little girl."

Wiley started undressing. "And what little girl is that?" he teased.

"The one we'll make someday."

He finished stripping and joined her on the bed. "Well, my dear, as Grandpappy Cyrus would have said, 'Why wait? There's no time like the present.'"

*Heart of the West*

A brand-new Harlequin continuity series
begins in July 1999
*with*

**Husband for Hire**
*by*
**Susan Wiggs**

*Beautician Twyla McCabe was Dear Abby
with a blow-dryer, listening to everyone else's
troubles. But now her well-meaning customers
have gone too far. No way was she attending
the Hell Creek High School Reunion with Rob
Carter, M.D. Who would believe a woman
who dyed hair for a living could be engaged
to such a hunk?*

*Here's a preview!*

# CHAPTER ONE

"THIS ISN'T FOR the masquerade. This is for me."

"What's for you?"

"This."

Rob didn't move fast, but with a straightforward deliberation she found oddly thrilling. He gripped Twyla by the upper arms and pulled her to him, covering her mouth with his.

*Dear God, a kiss.* She couldn't remember the last time a man had kissed her. And what a kiss. It was everything a kiss should be—sweet, flavored with strawberries and wine and driven by an underlying passion that she felt surging up through him, creating an answering need in her. She rested her hands on his shoulders and let her mouth soften, open. He felt wonderful beneath her hands, his muscles firm, his skin warm, his mouth... She just wanted to drown in him, drown in the passion. If he was faking his ardor, he was damned good. When he stopped kissing her, she stepped back. Her disbelieving fingers went to her mouth, lightly touching her moist, swollen lips.

"That...wasn't in the notes," she objected weakly.

"I like to ad-lib every once in a while."

"I need to sit down." Walking backward, never taking her eyes off him, she groped behind her and found the Adirondack-style porch swing. *Get a grip,* she told herself. *It was only a kiss.*

"I think," he said mildly, "it's time you told me just why you were so reluctant to come back here for the reunion."

"And why I had to bring a fake fiancé as a shield?"

Very casually, he draped his arm along the back of the porch swing. "I'm all ears, Twyla. Why'd I have to practically hog-tie you to get you back here?"

## COMING NEXT MONTH

### #741 THE BADGE AND THE BABY Alison Kent
**Bachelors & Babies**

Detective Joel Wolfsley was stuck with a baby! He adored his niece, but it was impossible to keep up with the munchkin while he was on crutches. Joel's delectable next-door neighbor came to the rescue. Willa Darling had a knack for mothering, even if her "babies" were of the canine variety.... She had a way with sexy uncles, too.

### #742 WHO'S THE BOSS? Jill Shalvis

Poor little rich girl Caitlin Taylor was in dire straits when her father died, leaving her nothing but an office job and a stack of bills. Her new boss was a computer whiz with an attitude, and no happier than Caitlin with the arrangement. If Joe hadn't worshiped Caitlin's father, he would have fired Calamity Jane on day one. But he let her stay, and soon he never wanted to let her go....

### #743 THE ROCKY RIDGE MAN Meredith March

Advertising exec Sonya Duncan had no use for cowboys, except as a filler for a pair of Rocky Ridge blue jeans. Just her luck that the only man whose gorgeous rear fit the bill happened to be the genuine article. Clint Silver was no more cooperative than a steer being branded, and Sonya had to use all her womanly wiles to corral the sexy rancher.

### #744 PURE TEMPTATION Vicki Lewis Thompson
**Blaze**

*Summer Project: Lose virginity.* At twenty-six, Tess Blakely's innocence was embarrassing. But growing up in a small town with four big brothers...well, she might as well have worn a chastity belt. She'd read all about sex—now she just needed to experience it with the right man. Her best friend, Jeremiah "Mac" MacDougal, was looking very tempting....